D1504358

PRINCESS KANDAKE
Warrior By Choice....Appointed to Rule

Stephanie Jefferson

For the very best grandchildren on the planet—mine. For my daughter. For my husband, For every girl who wonders if she can.

She looked into her brother's face. "Alara, I do not want to be queen," she said, standing over the pig's body. "The position I hope Great Mother chooses for me is Prime Warrior. I have good skills. You have seen them. With a little more time, they could be even better."

"That may be, but it is her decision. Who would you propose she name as the next ruler? Natasen? Tabiry?" When Kandake shook her head in the negative, he asked, "You cannot be thinking it should be me?"

"You would make a good king," she said.

Alara whistled the signal for the others to join them. Several men brought the cart forward and loaded Kandake's newest kill with the other carcasses.

"Thank you, but what we think does not matter." Alara pointed to the orange streaks of the setting sun. "It is time we head back." He accepted the reins of their horses from a servant.

"You just saw how well I track and shoot," Kandake continued as she vaulted to her horse's back. "I want to use these skills to protect the kingdom."

She and her brother turned their horses toward home.

"There is a caravan due to go out within a few days. If I go with it I could prove to Great Mother that I have the abilities to become Prime Warrior." She halted Strong Shadow to have her conversation with Alara.

"Have Father and Uncle Dakká decided who will accompany the caravan when it goes out to trade?" she asked, keeping her horse alongside his. "Do you suppose he would let me go?"

"Not this time, little sister. The rumors are these bandits are looking for more than to loot the caravan. We believe they are planning to blockade the trade route and exact usury to anyone who travels over it."

"They would not dare. Our warriors would cut them down before they got a foothold."

"That would work for one spot along the way, at least, but we could not protect the entire route. Each caravan will be accompanied by several of our warriors dressed as tradesmen and their apprentices."

"That would be perfect. It is what I have trained for and it will give me a chance to show Great Mother what I am capable of. I am a warrior; it is my duty to be there. It is what I have trained for."

"Father would never allow it." They rode through the entrance to the palace courtyard. "I doubt he would allow you to be in that type of situation. And you are to be established at the same time the next caravan is scheduled to leave."

"Alara, I need to go out with this one. It has to be before the ceremony, before Great Mother makes her decisions." Kandake pulled her face into the expression that usually got him to agree with her. "You could talk with Father, he listens to you. Get him to agree to let me go. We could have the ceremony when I get back."

"For that you need to speak with Father yourself." He reached across, placed his hand on hers. "It is your time to be Established as a woman and as daughter of the king. After that, tell Father what you want."

"By then it will be too late. Once I am Established, Great Mother will announce who she has named for which positions of court, including who will rule. What if she does not choose me as Prime Warrior? What if she chooses me for something else? That would ruin everything!" Kandake clasped her brother's arm, pleading. "You have to talk to Father now, before the ceremony; going out with the caravan will give me a little more time."

"How will that change anything?"

"Great Mother will have to name me as Prime Warrior once she sees what I can do. I really want that position." She gave his arm an extra squeeze. "Will you do it, please?"

"This is not something that can be done for you. You must do this for yourself."

"But I cannot." She added the argument that always worked with Alara. "You have to do it. You are my favorite brother."

"Of course you can do it." He smiled at her. "What if I was not here and for some reason I could not get back? Then what would you do?"

"I would come and find you. There is no other choice."

2

At the palace entrance, Kandake slid down from Strong Shadow's back and handed the reins to a waiting servant. She walked inside, whipped her cape from her shoulders and thrust it at the young man waiting there.

She knew there was no getting around the Establishing Ceremony, but she wanted to go out with that caravan more than anything right now. She hoped her mother would help her find a solution and went to find her.

The walls of the palace great room rose high and straight to the height of one and a half tall men above her reach. The hand-made bricks of rich, red-brown mud found in the distant valley were stacked one on top of the other. These also covered the floor, each block identical to the next, lying side-by-side in a neat pattern across the expanse. Columns, imitating the great palms of the valley reaching for the heavens, stretched to the ceiling.

Engravings of the history of the kingdom of Nubia graced the walls of the great hall. Images of past kings and queens stared back at Kandake as she walked by.

She turned into the passageway nearest her. Like many others throughout the palace, its walls bore illustrations of the great caravans loaded with the riches of Nubia: mounds of ivory tusks, stacks of animal hides, gold, ebony, and malachite.

This is where I am needed most. Her hand trailed along the etched scenes.

Kandake followed one of these corridors to her mother's rooms. She found Queen Sake reclining at a low table taking a light refreshment with her close friends. Plates of dates, figs, goat cheese and flat bread along with a pitcher of cool pomegranate juice lay before them.

"Mother, I need to speak with you," Kandake broke into their conversation.

"Kandake, your manners!" her mother said.

"Your pardon, please, Aunties," she said, bowing deeply. "Mother, may I please speak with you."

Her mother excused herself from her guests and ushered her daughter into her private chamber. They entered a room with tall windows open to take in the passing breeze. Lengths of colorful cloth hung from bronze rods providing privacy. Baskets of fruits and nuts graced the tabletops along with a decorative scattering of glass beads.

They seated themselves on a low cushioned bench. A young woman brought them some of the cool juice in shallow bowls. Kandake turned it in her hand, admiring the red base and blackened rim. Nubia had been making these vessels for generations. The design easily identified the item as belonging to the kingdom. In her hand was history and culture. This she was determined to protect.

Waiting until Kandake had been refreshed, her mother asked, "What is troubling you?"

"The caravan will leave in a few days to gather frankincense and I will not be able to go because of the ceremony," Kandake complained. "It has to be protected."

"That will be taken care of. But you are your father's youngest child. "The Establishing Ceremony is vital. It confirms you as King Amani's daughter, an heir to his throne." She loosened the binding that held Kandake's braids tied at the back of her neck. Pulling them forward, she laid them to rest on her daughter's shoulders, a more mature look.

"Your brothers and sister have been very patient. It is time to know who will rule Nubia after your father. Why should they have to wait while you go off with a caravan to the frankincense groves?"

"The wait would not be that long. They are only going to harvest the trees, not trade. I need the time to show Great Mother how my skills have advanced. I am hoping she will name me Prime Warrior."

"But it is not up to you. It is your grandmother's choice. What if she named you as queen? You would make a strong ruler." Queen Sake stroked her daughter's braided hair. "Besides, the ceremony confirms your entrance into womanhood."

"Why would I want to do that? My sister prances around like a queen bee holding court for her drones. And those stupid boys follow Tabiry wherever she goes." Kandake flapped and buzzed around the room making silly 'adoring' faces, mocking the boys that followed her sister.

"Tabiry bares her breasts to be sure no one mistakes her for a child. She wants the world to know she is a woman. She spends an entire day rubbing pieces of malachite against her palette until that stone is caked with the stuff. Just so she can layer it on her eyelids. And have you seen the amount of kohl she sketches around her eyes? The way she applies it cannot be for protection from the sun's glare. It is all because she has begun taking suitors, ugh!" Kandake continued. "She wants marriage and children. So do Alara and Natasen. I am not sure if that is for me."

"Do you plan to hold onto your childhood forever?" her mother asked. The sound of worry in her voice matched the crease of concern between her brows.

"No, Mother. I will be a woman—but as a warrior."

3

"No one seems to understand," Kandake muttered as she drove herself, perfecting her holds on the man-shaped, straw-filled figure that served as her sparring partner.

She worked in the center of the training room of the warrior compound. It was a large square space with walls covered in weapons of all kinds used for practice and instruction. Kandake flipped the practice dummy over her shoulder, which was the weight of a large man.

"If this is what I want, where is the harm in that?" She pounced on the figure, grasped its arm and milked it for the knife she pretended it held. "Here is where my talents lie."

Sucking down great gulps of air, sweat seeping from every pore, Kandake walked past tall narrow windows and scores of training figures. Some hung from stands and others fastened to frames. She trudged to the large clay vessel filled with drinking water standing at the back of the room.

"A ritual is not necessary to tell me who my father is." She drank a second cup. "I know who he is."

She mopped her drenched skin with a square of absorbent hide and returned to her practice, this time paying close attention to her footwork.

During the execution of a particularly difficult hold, the sound of sandals scuffing over the floor broke her concentration. She turned.

"Why are you so angry?" Ezena, Kandake's closest friend, stepped onto the sparring floor. "You are tearing the head off that." She pointed to the dummy Kandake had in a stranglehold.

"They expect me to go through with the Establishing Ceremony within the next few days. I want to be where I am needed, protecting the caravans that are in danger of attack. That is where a warrior should go, not waiting around to be declared someone's daughter."

"That is not going to happen. You just had your fourteenth birthday. Your mother is obligated to present you to confirm your position as heir to your father's throne."

Kandake dropped the dummy and faced her friend. "I have no interest in being queen. This is what I am good at." She dealt the practice figure a deadly blow. "Can a queen do this? Or use any of these?" She swept her hand around the weapon-covered walls. "My heart is in this, what I was designed to do— protect this kingdom." Her strike to the dummy took its head off and exploded its chest. "I need the time to show Great Mother."

"The ceremony is not only about the throne. It is where you take your womanhood. You will not be able to take suitors without doing it."

"Suitors? Why would I want to do that? I am not my sister." Kandake pulled her knife from its scabbard, advanced on another training figure—this one fastened to a frame.

"That is not what I am saying. You are nothing like her. One day you will want to get married or have children. You cannot do either without going through the ceremony."

"I can do both as a warrior."

"Yes, but you cannot if you are still a child."

Kandake paused. She let her shoulders fall and turned to face her friend. "I would not mind going through the ceremony if that was all there was to it. But if I am declared a woman and my father's child, Great Mother could name me as his successor. I do not want to be HIS successor I want to be Uncle Dakká's."

Ezena put a comforting hand on her friend's arm. "You would do well as Prime Warrior. But if you are not an heir that cannot happen."

Ezena's words encouraged her. She met her friend's gaze. "I will work harder. Improve my skills. Show Great Mother that I can protect Nubia. Already my arrows strike wherever I aim."

Kandake returned to the standing vessel of water. She filled the clay cup and drank deeply, then poured the remainder over her head and dried herself off with the piece of hide. She looked around the area, envisioning herself teaching young warriors, assessing the skills of the apprentices and assigning them to their first watches, and plotting wartime strategies if it came to that. *This is where I belong. I will show Uncle Dakká and Great Mother that I am worthy of following him.* Her heart filled with greater determination.

"I have been watching you," Ezena said. "It looks like you have mastered the footing on that last pass. That one always tangles me up. Kurru has walked me through it more times than I can count." She held up the small bundle she carried. "Are you ready to stop for a while? I brought salted fish and a few honeyed dates."

Kandake and her friend walked out of the building and took a seat in the shade of one of its walls.

"Did you really think you could avoid the ceremony?" Ezena asked.

"No, but I had hoped that I could postpone it." She bit into the portion of fish Ezena shared with her. "I just wanted enough time to go out with the caravan. How is your sister?" she asked, changing the subject.

"She is doing well. Her belly is growing. Her husband struts around like a preening rooster."

"Can you blame him? He has fathered ten children. All of them live and are strong." She popped a date into her mouth, savored the sweetness. It complimented the salty fish. "I noticed that you have begun baring your breasts. Why have you changed?"

Ezena looked away from Kandake.

"Who is he?" Kandake teased. "Who in this kingdom could interest you enough to consider marriage?"

"I have been thinking about Nateka, Kashta's oldest son."

"Nateka, but he is an artisan. You would marry someone other than a warrior?"

"Warriors are not the only strong men in Nubia."

"Are you changing your mind about all of this, what you have worked for?" Kandake waved her hand indicating the warrior's compound. "You succeed to apprentice level only to give it up?" Kandake stared at Ezena, wondering what would cause her friend to choose something else.

"Why would that have to change? Most of our warriors are married."

"You have never talked about marriage before, and I know you have not mentioned Nateka."

"He is the perfect choice for me. He is strong—no one could ever doubt his courage. He prefers to make things. His ironwork and his arrowheads are the best in the kingdom."

Kandake watched her friend's face as she described the young man. She saw tenderness mixed with determination. Every time Ezena said his name, light sparked her eyes and a smile played at the corners of her mouth. "You have been receiving his company. Admit it."

Ezena lost the struggle of keeping the smile from her lips. "Yes," she said, nodding. "But he has visited our home only once."

"Will you marry him?"

"I said, I have only had the one visit and I have not yet shared time with other suitors. How could I choose from that?"

Kandake continued to watch her friend's face. *You may have only received him the one time, but I doubt any others will stand a chance.* "I am happy for you," she said.

14

"What about you?" Ezena asked. "Will you receive suitors after the ceremony?"

"I do not believe that is for me. But if it were, I am sure I would want a warrior to present himself. You have seen Tabiry and her entourage. If anyone dared to act like that around me, I would probably use him for practice." She pointed back toward the sparring floor. "For now there is only room in my life for one thing—the position of Nubia's Prime Warrior."

.

4

"Great Mother," Kandake said. "You sent for me?" She knelt before her grandmother, back erect, head bowed with her eyes lowered in a pose of respect for the woman before her.

"Come, sit with me." Her grandmother patted the pillows next to hers. "We need to talk."

Kandake compared these rooms with her mother's. The structure was the same, but the colors and furnishings were very different. Her mother favored cushioned benches and wooden tables. Here, the choice was lush pillows of assorted shapes and sizes.

About the room stood petite tables of braided reeds. On them, small bronze plates displayed multicolored glass beads or metal figurines. On a table in the far corner, her grandmother burned incense, adding the light fragrance of frankincense to the room.

Kandake took the large red cushion, seating herself next to the gold one of her grandmother. She plucked a few nuts from the tabletop basket nearby.

"What is this I hear about you not wanting to be

established as your father's daughter?"

"It is not that," Kandake said, shifting the nuts to her cheek. "It is everything that comes with it. Baring my breasts, taking suitors, knowing you will announce father's successor."

"Do you believe you must do it all immediately? Bare your breasts when you are ready." Great Mother took Kandake's chin in her hand. "Tabiry tried to embrace all of her womanhood in one day. She was eager to become a woman well before her establishing. She loves the attention of suitors. This will make it hard for her to settle on just one."

"I am not like my sister. She wants to be fawned over, taken care of like a child. I do not want any of that."

"No. The two of you are very different." Great Mother crossed to the window. "Come, look at what I see."

Kandake joined her.

"Look out on the beauty of Nubia," her grandmother continued. She pulled the drapery away to give them a clear view. "The land we rule is lush. Look at our herds. The cattle are fat and healthy. The Nile brings us riches and carries our trade to far away places so our people prosper and are happy. Who could not love this kingdom?"

Kandake watched where her grandmother pointed. Pride filled her as she gazed out over the fields and herds. This was a territory worth protecting. A kingdom she could give her life for. "Oh, but I do, Great Mother. I love our home and everything in it. I plan to be its greatest warrior. If I am chosen as Prime, it would be my responsibility to safeguard all of this, everything that makes Nubia great. I want that responsibility." She turned to face her grandmother. "Escorting the caravan is a way to begin. I am strong. I can ride. Ask Uncle Dakká. He will tell you that my arrow strikes whatever my eye sees."

"I have spoken with your uncle. He assures me that you are, by far, one of his best students. Together, you and Natasen have shown greater skill than any of the other apprentices, and some of your skills rival those of the senior warriors."

"Then you know I can do this, protect the caravan. If father lets me go with them, he would see it, too. Please talk to him. He will listen to you."

"No, precious child." Her grandmother stroked her face. "Not this time. You must be here for the ceremony. Your brothers and sister have been waiting to know my decision."

"You could tell them without me. Your decision does not have to involve me. I do not even have to be Prime. Just being a warrior of the kingdom is enough for me."

Great Mother rested her hand on Kandake's shoulder, quieting her granddaughter's arguments.

"The naming cannot take place until the king's last child is established," she said. "And that is you."

"But—"

"No buts." She turned and looked out of the window. The two were silent for a time, gazing out onto the lands and peoples of Nubia.

Is there anyone who understands? Being a warrior is not something I want to do. It is who I am.

"Great Mother," Kandake said, with a slow exhale of breath and fall of her shoulders. "If it were left to me, I would choose to be a warrior over everything else."

Her grandmother wrapped an arm around Kandake's shoulders, gave them a gentle squeeze, and said, "I know, strong child, but it is more often that life chooses for us."

5

On the portico outside the great hall of the palace, King Amani stood next to his raised throne constructed of polished ebony. Large ivory tusks bearing the carved images of Nubia's rulers of the past decorated his throne. He wore lengths of fabric dyed in bold colors of green, gold, blue and brown, draped from his waist to mid-calf, reflecting the richness of Nubia.

His brothers, Prince Dakká and Prince Naqa stood in the places of honor on either side of him. One step behind Prince Dakká, but closer to the king stood Princess Alodia, the king's only sister. On the dais, presented to all of Nubia, the royal family stood radiant in beauty and strength.

The citizenry crowded themselves around the boundaries of the porch, straining to get the best spot to watch the ceremony. The sun was kind today and gentle breezes from the Nile brought a reprieve from the press of bodies.

A small band of women approached the king, stopping at the very center of the court. The women at the front of the group stepped away, revealing the two women they surrounded. The party lowered themselves, touching one knee to the ground, with backs erect and heads bowed in a show of respect.

"What have you come for?" King Amani bellowed in a voice that carried to the last row of onlookers.

"I, the wife of your heart, Queen Sake of Nubia, have brought you your last child," Kandake's mother responded in the traditional manner.

"If that is so, let me see her."

Kandake, kneeling beside her mother, covered with a veil of sheer crimson gauze, raised her head. King Amani left his throne striding to the place where she was bowed. Bare to the waist, his skin glistened in the sunlight. Dark as the earth he trod, King Amani's coloring was a testament to the legend of Nubia being highly favored by their god. Skin kissed by the sun would forever be their proof of blessing.

He reached down and removed the covering from his daughter. "What is this?" he roared. "You said you had brought me my last child—this is a woman."

Kandake arose, nearly matching her father's height. She stood before him with breasts bared, bow and quiver across her back, a sling draped at her hip, and a long spear in her hand, the trappings of a warrior. She lifted her chin and spoke in a voice for all to hear.

"I am Kandake, daughter of King Amani,

princess of Nubia. Father, you came looking for a child, but the veil revealed a woman. I stand here a warrior, one warrior that will protect Nubia, and all that is hers, with my life."

King Amani stepped backwards in mock surprise of the strength of the words Kandake flung at him. A slow smile crept across his face as pride filled his eyes. At his signal, her brothers and sister joined him. "You speak like the daughter of a king," he said, embracing her.

King Amani took the hand of Kandake's mother and lifted her to her feet. "My Queen," he said. "You have given me strong children, all of them. I am in your debt." He bowed in respect to her, dipping his knee to the ground.

"These are the children of Amani, King of Nubia," he announced to the crowd, rising. "Heirs to my throne."

Cheers broke out throughout the crowd of citizens gathered for the ceremony. Servants brought long tables onto the portico. They covered the tops of these with meats, fruits, vegetables, bread, and cheeses. Pitchers of water, fruit juice, and fermented grains were on hand. All of Nubia celebrated the king's fortune.

Kandake filled her plate with selections from each platter. She chose a seat on the bench next to Alara. Once settled, a servant filled her cup with cool fruit juice.

"You did well," Alara said, giving her shoulder an encouraging squeeze.

"That part was not hard," she answered,

smiling at him. "But it will be annoying to have boys buzzing around me like so many flies."

"Just ignore them like you always have." He grinned and filled his mouth with meat and herbs.

"Sorry you did not get to go out with the caravan," Natasen offered. "I am sure Father will let you go with the next one. I am hoping to get assigned to one of them myself. No caravans will be traveling without guards anymore. That makes it a certainty that we will each get a chance."

Natasen's sentiments heartened her. Of the four of them, he had a warrior's heart like her own. She completed the celebratory meal with her family, all the while laughing and participating in the conversation with them, but anxiety for what lay ahead gnawed at her heart and mind.

As the feasting came to an end, the servants cleared away the last of the meal's clutter. King Amani returned to his throne. His mother walked to the center of the courtyard carrying a large four-sided earthen vessel, a box with no openings. The likeness of the present and past rulers of Nubia had been carved into three sides of the box: King Amani; his father, King Naqa; and King Naqa's mother, Queen Tabiry. The fourth side was blank, waiting for the face of the ruler that would follow Amani.

All eyes rested on Nubia's Great Mother, the mother of the king. Silence fell on everyone within the portico. She took measured and deliberate steps toward the king, the box extended from her with strong arms.

This is the hard part. Kandake felt each footfall as her grandmother approached the throne. Her eyes filled with the vision of her future contained within that baked brown box. This moment embraced the most difficult task she had faced in her life. No test of discipline or endurance that Uncle Dakká had ever dreamed up in her training as a warrior could compare with this moment. Now that she had been Established as the king's daughter and as a Nubian woman, the weight of what was to come sat heavily upon her shoulders and gripped her heart. The next few moments would determine the path of her life.

Please, do not let my name be on the gold tablet, she prayed to anyone that might be listening. *Let me serve as a warrior. Let my cartouche be clay. Please say that I will be Prime.*

Kandake watched her grandmother set the clay box at the feet of the king. Her heart felt the blow Uncle Dakká delivered, shattering its top. Though her mind screamed 'run,' her feet refused to obey. She could not tear her eyes away as he checked the back of each cartouche for her grandmother's seal. That done, he handed them off to the king's advisor, her Aunt Alodia.

Aunt Alodia examined the name on each cartouche and handed the stack to the king. Kandake could not breathe watching her father read each one. He smiled as he came to the last in the stack, the gold cartouche that named his successor.

Not me. Please, not me.

6

Kandake sat in the silence watching her father with the tablets in his hand. He seemed to be waiting for something. She felt time sludge by—measuring an eternity. *I cannot take it. Will this never end?*

At last, King Amani rose from his throne. He walked to the edge of the dais and addressed his mother, but his voice could be heard in the valley beyond.

"You have shown me the future of Nubia. Great Mother, you have guaranteed a kingdom of strength. Thank you for your gift." He walked back across the platform and handed the stack to his wife. "Queen of my heart, look and see the future of Nubia."

Kandake watched her mother examine the clay and gold tablets. She searched her face for a hint at whose name was inscribed on each one. When her mother read the name on the tablet of gold, Kandake averted her eyes. She feared what she might read into her mother's expression.

King Amani took possession of the slabs once more and passed one to each of his brothers and one to his sister. The golden cartouche he kept for himself.

"Children of Amani, King of Nubia, present yourselves," his voice rang throughout the courtyard.

Kandake stood and walked forward with the others. The space from her seat to the foot of the raised podium felt endless. The ground clung to each of her feet as she lifted them to move forward. A knotted mess sat in the place her stomach usually resided. A quick glance at her siblings' faces told her that they shared an equally difficult journey. Natasen, whose stride always bounded like that of a new lamb, was heavy, lacking its usual energy. Alara wore a face of stone, devoid of expression. And her sister, Tabiry, schooled her features to a studied neutral.

I am a daughter of the king, Kandake reminded herself taking careful steps leading up the dais. *I am warrior strong. I will survive whatever life chooses for me.* With careful steps, she climbed the dais.

When they had placed themselves before their father, Kandake scrutinized his face as he acknowledged each one of his children. She could not read him. *If I do not know soon, my heart will explode from my chest.* At the king's nod, Uncle Naqa stepped forward.

"I present to you the future of Nubia's wealth," Uncle Naqa announced. His voice, cool as a refreshing breeze, carried to eager ears awaiting his proclamation. "It has been my honor to assure the kingdom's prosperity. When the next to rule assumes the throne the treasure will continue to abound. Our Great Mother has seen to it."

Uncle Naqa came to face the row of King Amani's children. He handed the cartouche he held to

Tabiry. The bland expression she had been holding split into a bold grin as her uncle placed the conferring kiss upon her brow. She held the clay tablet high above her head for all to witness her good fortune.

"I present to you, Tabiry, the Protector of Nubia's Wealth."

Kandake saw her sister's body relax. Her happiness for Tabiry was tarnished by her own growing tension.

That is fine by me. That was not a position I wanted. It really does suit Tabiry. Her mind has always been directed toward trade.

"I present to you the future of Nubia's strength," Uncle Dakká declared, stepping forward. "It has been my honor to protect this kingdom, to keep it strong by training its warriors. This is certain in the next reign. Our Great Mother has secured this."

Uncle Dakká strode to Natasen, handing him the slab bearing his name. Natasen accepted it, only just containing his excitement when his brow was kissed, his body vibrated with it. He shoved the piece of baked clay high into the air above his head.

"This is Nubia's protection and strength. Our next Prime Warrior will ensure it."

Kandake did her best to keep her shoulders from sagging. Her eyes stung as they swept over her brother, assessing his training-hardened body for flaws. She examined him for any signs of weakness. There were none. *He has earned it,* she reminded herself and forced her face to smile at his good fortune. The faces of Alara and Tabiry shared in it with him. But this was the cartouche she had wanted as her own.

This is too hard. That one should have been mine. I wanted to be Prime. Kandake pushed her mind and body through a quick discipline exercise and brought herself to calm. *Advisor would not be so bad. I would still travel to other kingdoms and I could use my skills to protect the king along with Natasen. Advisor could be good.* Kandake had just about quieted her worry when she heard her aunt's rich voice address the court.

"I present to you the Wisdom of Nubia," Aunt Alodia intoned, her presence a blend of grace and beauty. She stood as tall as her brother, the king, and her skin just as dark. The princess possessed a gentle manner and an unyielding spirit and temperament. "It has been my honor to serve Nubia with discernment and understanding. This will only increase in the next rule. Our Great Mother has made it so."

Kandake waited for her aunt to come to her. She all but held her hand out as her aunt advanced beyond her to her brother, Alara. Surprise and pleasure mingled on her brother's face as his shoulders visibly relaxed.

He accepted his cartouche from his aunt's hand.

No! Kandake's mind screamed. *NO!*

Her aunt kissed his forehead, conferring the position upon Alara. He raised the symbol and waved it in obvious delight.

No, no, no, no, no, swam across her consciousness.

King Amani left his place before the throne. Proud, measured strides took him to the position in front of his youngest daughter. Kandake forced her eyes to hold with his. Pulling her shoulders back, she elevated her chin determined to meet what life had given her.

"I present to you the future of this kingdom," King Amani proclaimed with his hand beneath Kandake's chin. "The richness of Nubia's people, strength, and wealth are bound within one person."

It took all of Kandake's strength not to wrench her chin from her father's grasp. Bone and muscle tensed. Her heart begged her to run.

"That person rules, protects, and guides the kingdom and represents her to the world beyond our borders. Thank you, Great Mother, for ensuring that Nubia will be all that she ever was, and more." He held the golden cartouche above Kandake's head for everyone to see. "Before you stands the next Queen of Nubia!"

Deafened by the roar of the crowd, Kandake could not hear what her father was saying, but the pride in his eyes spoke volumes. He placed the conferring kiss upon her brow.

Alara pounded her on the back, sporting a grin that doubled the width of his face. Natasen cheered her, but he was kind enough to mouth 'I am sorry.' And Tabiry, her face was carefully neutral—again.

7

Kandake looked around her, ears ringing with cheers, whistles, and excited calls. All of the faces matched the sounds surrounding her, except Tabiry's. Their eyes locked, Kandake could read nothing from her sister's expression. She had the distinct feeling her sister was not pleased with their grandmother's choice, but neither was she.

Her father led her to the bench that had been placed in front of his throne. She could hear his voice, but her mind was on Tabiry. She missed what he was saying. Under her grandmother's supervision, Kandake was lowered onto the seat of honor.

A craftsman came forward and removed the bronze circlet of bells from her ankle. These marked Kandake and her siblings as the children of the king of Nubia. The artisan gave it to Uncle Dakká who destroyed the circlet and bells and gave the mangled metal to Great Mother.

For protection from the heat, heavy fabric stacked with sandwiched layers of sand and leaf-wrapped metal was wound around Kandake's leg. An apprentice to the craftmaster held them in place. The craftmaster took a length of thick gold wire. He softened the section by passing it through a bed of white-hot coals resting on fired, clay bricks. Another apprentice fanned the embers, maintaining its great heat.

He pulled the gold from the flame, its glow a bright orange-red. With the hot wire sandwich between layers of fabric, he placed it at the back of Kandake's protected leg. With one slow motion, he bent it into a loop. Over one open end he slid several golden bells. Spacing in between them he used tiny glass beads. With great skill, the craftmaster fused the two ends together. Closing the circle marked Kandake as the next to ascend to the throne of Nubia.

I do not want this. I never wanted this. I want to protect Nubia, but not like this. Not as queen.

Kandake's foot was doused with cold water from the Nile, cooling the metal, protecting her skin. Setting her foot on the floor of the dais brought the bells' delicate tinkle to life striking against one another. She rose from the bench and stood alongside her father. A cheer went up from the crowd before everyone lowered themselves in a show of respect for the present and future rulers of Nubia.

Great Mother stepped to Kandake and wrapped the braid closest to her right ear with thin gold wire. Its tail ended with three golden bells with their graceful tones of gold upon gold, further marking her granddaughter as heir to the throne. "Your desire was to protect Nubia as a warrior," her grandmother said, pride filling her voice. "Now you can protect her as queen."

"Great Mother, you chose what you believe is best for Nubia," Kandake told her, strength wrapping each word. "I will choose what is best for me. I accept that I will be Nubia's queen, but I will be her warrior queen."

8

"I knew this would happen," Kandake told Ezena. She stretched her legs out, sitting beside her friend. Spending time together after dinner had been a ritual they shared since they had begun warrior training. The evening air was pleasant and clear. "I never wanted to be queen."

"I know," Ezena said, sympathy filling her words. "What will you do?"

"Rule when the time comes. It has not been a whole week and already Father has rearranged my life. Most mornings I spend studying with him about our laws, the expectations of my position as queen, and learning the intricate relationships between Nubia and other kingdoms. In the afternoon, I sit with him beside his throne observing how he manages the kingdom and disputes that come to his attention."

"What about your training as a warrior? Will you have to stop?"

"No!" Kandake's voice was sharp. "They cannot make me. That will never change." She turned to face her friend. "I will continue the usual training on the mornings that I do not meet with Father. When morning practice is not possible, I will train with Uncle Dakká in the afternoon."

"That makes for a very long day," her friend said, shaking her head.

"It is the only time I can train. I will not give it up." She looked at Ezena. "Nothing will keep me from being the best warrior I can be." She clenched her fists; her back was rigid with determination.

The girls sat in silence, gazing at the stars of the darkened sky. The aromas of healthy cattle and the sounds of the Nile lapping at the edges of the shoreline filled the evening air.

"Ezena, you have to promise me something."

"What is it?"

"Promise that you will always be my friend, even when I rule."

"Of course. Who else is going tell you when you are being stubborn or that your footwork is sloppy?"

Kandake rose and walked to the edge of the river. Removing her sandals, she pressed her feet into the cool mud, enjoying the squish of it between her toes. She bent down and sketched figures on the wet ground.

"I wish I knew why Great Mother chose me."

"Have you asked her?"

"I do not know what to say."

"That is a first. You have an opinion about everything."

"It is just that—"

"You are angry with her."

"Not really." Kandake saw the doubt in her friend's eyes. "Maybe I am, but I am more disappointed than angry, more confused than disappointed. She should have chosen Alara."

"Why?"

"Because he is the logical choice. Alara is very even-tempered, he forgives easily, and he is generous with his praise and support. All of the characteristics I believe would make a good ruler. That is not who I am."

"What if Great Mother chose you because you are not like your brother? What if she selected you because Nubia needs something different, someone with a different kind of strength?"

"Then what is she hoping that I will become? I do not know how to be anything other than what I am—a warrior."

After their visit, Kandake made her way to her rooms, ruminating over Great Mother's choice. Natasen sat on the bench by a window waiting for her.

"I have been waiting so long," he said as she entered. "I thought maybe you had decided to stay the night with Ezena."

"What do you want?" She was trying to act as if nothing had changed, but she heard the sting of her voice.

"I wanted to come and apologize. I know you hoped to be named Prime as much as I did."

"I am not angry with you. I did want it, but you deserve it just as much. I only wish I could understand Great Mother's choice."

"Who should she have chosen? Tabiry?"

Kandake giggled at the face her brother made and wondered if hers held the same expression. *Tabiry as queen? Never*! "Probably not, but I could understand if she had chosen Alara."

"But she did not choose him. You are her choice. Like it or not, you are our next queen."

"I am not certain that I will ever like it." She flopped onto a nearby chair. "How are you enjoying the idea of being Prime? Does it feel as wonderful as I dreamed?"

"It would be if Uncle Dakká was not cramming strikes and strategies into my head. It has not been a full week yet, and I have already worked harder than any two weeks."

"Father is doing the same with me. Who knew there would be so much to learn?"

Natasen crossed the room and knelt in front of his sister. "I want you to know that I think you would have been an excellent choice for Prime. You are becoming a fine warrior."

"Thank you for that." She leaned forward and touched her forehead to his. A gesture of closeness they shared since they were small children. "I am sure Tabiry is as happy with her position as a giraffe in a stand of acacias."

"Great Mother's choice is a perfect match. No one pays more attention to trade and the value of wares than she does."

For a moment the air between them lightened. The mental pictures she created of Tabiry wrangling better trade agreements with other kingdoms and the pleasure she would take in squeezing them for whatever she could had Kandake chuckling.

"Alara seems to be as pleased about his

appointment," Natasen added.

"It would seem that everyone else is pleased with what Great Mother chose for them except me." Kandake slumped against the back of her chair, her moment of amusement ended. "I always knew it could happen. Only, I had hoped it would not."

"I really am sorry."

"We need to talk about something else."

"I have been assigned to go out with the next caravan. Has your time to be on escort been arranged yet?"

"No, but Father says he will let me go soon," she said, feeling a little annoyed. "He wants me to get adjusted to my study schedule before I interrupt it with such a journey. He makes it sound like there is nothing useful I can learn from escorting the caravan."

"Do not worry, little sister. You will get your turn."

"Yes, but when?" Kandake sprang out of the chair, almost knocking her brother over. She planted her feet and all but shouted, "Escorting the caravans is not only important for their protection and for Nubia's trade. It is an important part of my training, too. I did not have a choice about being queen, but I do have one about being a warrior. Father, and everyone else, will have to accept that I plan to do both."

9

"But she is only fourteen," Kandake heard Tabiry say, her voice dripping with undisguised disapproval. "Alara is the oldest. Great Mother should have chosen him." Someone murmured a response, but she could not make out what they had said or who had said it.

Kandake agreed. *I wish she had chosen Alara, too. But she did not. She chose me.* Moving closer to hear more of the conversation, she inched along the wall. She flexed her foot, tucking the bells into the fold of skin at her ankle, keeping them quiet.

"What kind of queen will she make for Nubia?" Tabiry ranted. "You have seen her. She prefers to hunt. She practices her battle skills all day."

It is one thing for me to wonder about Great Mother's choice, but for it to be questioned by someone like her….

Kandake heard footsteps coming toward the doorway and flattened herself against the wall. No one exited the room, but Tabiry continued.

"She does not sit with Aunt Alodia like Alara does. She is off training in the warrior compound. Kandake will bring war to Nubia. You remember I warned you."

"How is it you have not noticed?" This was Natasen's strong, steady voice. "War is already coming to Nubia. Bandits challenge our caravans because of the rumors that Assyria may be attacking Egypt. If it is not Assyria, it is likely Persia. It is not important who it is. If another kingdom attacks our neighbor—Great Mother was right. Nubia will need a strong leader."

"Why am I bothering to talk to you," Tabiry huffed. "You are just as bad as she is."

"Why are you questioning Great Mother, she—"

Kandake let the tinkle of her bells warn them that she was near before entering the room.

"Hello, my sister, the warrior queen." The warmth in Natasen's voice welcomed her.

"Kandake," Tabiry said, her features no longer neutral. Her mouth twisted like she had taken a bite of bitter herbs.

"I am going for a swim," Kandake told her brother. "Do you want to come with me?"

"I would think you would have more important things to do," Tabiry said. "Like maybe learn some wisdom from Aunt Alodia?"

"I have been working with Father all morning. It is time for a break."

"I would love to swim," Natasen said. He set aside the bowstring he had been working on, entwining two strands for greater strength. "But I can only go for a short time. Uncle Dakká has some strategies he wants me to study. Tabiry, are you coming?"

"No. I do not have time for play." She left them and turned in the direction of their mother's rooms.

"Why is she so angry with me? Did she want to be queen so badly?" Kandake asked, staring after her sister as they headed for their swim.

"Do not listen to her. She thinks you are too much like me to rule," he said, pointing to the knife she wore on her right hip. It was the same place he wore his. Natasen had given Kandake the knife for her twelfth birthday. Its hilt, wrapped with a leather thong, was topped with a cabochon of carnelian.

Natasen made a dismissive gesture toward their older sister's back. Placing gentle pressure on Kandake's elbow, he urged her onto the path that led to the Nile. It took them past the potter's yard. His apprentices tread the clay with their bare feet.

The jingle of bells of the two royals announced their presence, eliciting the acknowledgement of those they passed. The potter lowered himself to a respectful knee, interrupting his chore of adding sand to the mix.

"Why do you think it bothers her so much?" Kandake asked. She accepted the show of respect from the citizens with a nod of her head.

"She is worried that a warrior on the throne could bring war to Nubia."

"Do you think she is right?"

Natasen shrugged. "War could come to Nubia no matter who sits on the throne. A warrior queen might give enemies a second thought about attacking or give our kingdom an advantage."

Kandake took in everything around her on their way to the water. Everyone she passed seemed pleased to see her. They honored her by lowering themselves and where appropriate she smiled in return. A small girl sitting on a woven mat with her mother ran to Kandake. She offered her a half-eaten, honeyed fig. Kandake accepted the gift, took a tiny bite and gave it back to the child.

"You see?" her brother pointed out. "Not everyone shares Tabiry's worries." Kandake chewed the sweet treat with its sand-encrusted flesh, returning her brother's smile.

The two undressed in the reeds down to their undergarments and entered the cool water. They swam past a smallish pond in which workers were retting flax for linen. Further on, cattle waded along the river's edge for watering and brother and sister whistled their greetings to those tending them. Kandake rolled onto her back and floated near the shoreline.

"Why do you think Great Mother chose me?" she asked Natasen. "Part of me agrees with Tabiry. I still think she should have chosen Alara."

"Do you remember, about four years ago?" Natasen stroked to bring himself alongside his sister. "There was that old woman who had a fever. She believed that her precious goat was her dead husband come back to steal from her."

Kandake brought back the memory. The woman had been delirious with fever, swinging an ax. Her target was the goat, but would also swing it at anyone that tried to stop her.

Natasen's hands sculled lazy circles keeping him near his sister in the water. "She would have killed the animal if you had not agreed to watch him all night."

"But that goat was the prize of her flock. If she had killed him, there would have been no lambs the following spring."

"True, but you were not even nine and you sat up all night. Then the next year Tabiry slept on her wet hair without braiding it. The curls had wrapped around themselves and dried there, locked strand-to-strand. What a tangled mess!"

Kandake rolled over in the water. "I worked with Mother all morning and most of the afternoon to help her get all of the knots out of Tabiry's hair." Kandake splashed her brother, giggling. "Mother threatened to cut her hair off and Tabiry wailed instead of helping us."

"And last week when we were fishing, you pretended to have confused your full net with that little boy's empty one."

"You saw his face. How could I let him go home with an empty net when he had promised his father he would provide their family's evening meal?"

"What about on our way here? You took a bite of that little girl's sweet treat. It was covered with sand. How many times do you think she dropped it? That is why Great Mother chose you. You love Nubia."

"So do you," Kandake said. She used her tongue to remove the last of the fig's grit from her teeth. "So does Tabiry, for that matter."

"But you love her people. You never think of yourself, first. You love Nubia's people most. Give yourself time, you will see Great Mother was right."

_10_

Weeks had passed since the ceremony naming Kandake as Nubia's next queen. She entered the council chamber off the throne room, the area King Amani used to discuss important matters. It was constructed of the same red-brown brick as the rest of the building. The room's main furnishing, a sturdy table of cedar inlaid with a map of Nubia and the surrounding areas. Next to it stood her father and Uncle Dakká, speaking in low voices and pointing at various locations on the map.

"Father, please," Kandake said. "I really need to speak with you."

"One moment. Your uncle and I must finish this so that the caravan can leave."

"That is what I need to speak with you about. I want to go out with it."

"Not this time." He continued to study the map. "Maybe the next one."

"You have said that about every one that has left so far. All of the apprentices have had an opportunity to go except me. Even Natasen has gone."

"She is right, My King." Uncle Dakká came to her

defense. "You have to let her go sometime. Unless you want her training to be less than adequate, she must take her turn escorting the caravans."

"You know that is not what I want," King Amani hedged. "Maybe with the next one."

"No, Amani, it has to be this one."

"But the bandits—"

"She will be safe. And if it makes you feel any better, I am planning to go along on this one myself."

Kandake watched her father and uncle wrangle back and forth. She knew her father could be stubborn, but so could her uncle. Every argument her father raised to keep her here, her uncle raised two more to let her go.

Please, Father, Kandake pleaded within. *Listen to Uncle. You have to let me go.*

They stopped talking. Kandake scrutinized her father's face. It twisted with displeasure. He paced back and forth. On his third trip away from his brother, he seemed to make up his mind. Turning to face Uncle Dakká, he said, "You are certain you are going on this trip?"

"Yes," her uncle answered.

"And you will keep her safe?"

"Yes."

"Then I will let her go."

"Thank you, thank you," Kandake said, throwing herself at her father. "Thank you, thank you." She turned and attacked her uncle with the same exuberance.

"The caravan leaves within the hour," her uncle told her. "You will need your sling, bow, and traveling cape. And go to the tanner, she has prepared something special for you. You will need that, too."

Kandake sprinted to gather her things before her father had a chance to change his mind. She ran to her rooms. Snatching up a small pouch, she poured its contents on the tabletop. She lifted the leather straps that formed her sling. She tested them for strength. The tethers were strong. She counted the small smooth stones to be sure there would be plenty, if needed. She returned the contents to the pouch and tied it to the hip opposite her knife. Kandake looped her bow over her shoulder so that it fell comfortably at her back. Counting the arrows in her quiver, she added an extra bowstring and a few fletches for good measure. She grabbed her travel cape and ran to her mother's rooms to say goodbye.

"I came to tell you that I am going with the caravan," Kandake told her mother, who was braiding her sister's hair.

"Your father finally consented to let you go?" Queen Sake asked, smiling. "I never thought he would agree to it."

"It was not easy. Uncle Dakká had to convince him."

"I agree with Father. You should be here studying instead of off somewhere playing warrior," Tabiry said. She sat on the floor between her mother's knees.

"Tabiry! Show respect," their mother said.

"Why? She is not queen, yet." Tabiry said. "What could Great Mother have been thinking, choosing her?"

"You question Great Mother's wisdom?" their

mother scolded. "Tabiry, at times you go too far."

"Are you saying your choice would have been better?" Kandake glared down at her. "I do not know what she was thinking, but I know her decision is best for Nubia. Not because she chose me, but because she loves this kingdom. Do you?" Taking a deep breath, she calmed herself, then stepped past her sister. She removed her bow and quiver, laid these aside with her cape, and knelt at her mother's side with her head bowed. "I came to ask you to bless my journey," Kandake whispered.

"I ask that you remember who you are while you are gone, Princess Kandake." Her mother spoke in a soft, compelling voice, stroking Kandake's head and shoulders. "Be wise, be strong, return safely to those who love you." She kissed the top of Kandake's forehead.

Kandake rose. Circling her arms about her mother's neck, she whispered, "I will not let you down. I will remember." She snatched up her bow, quiver, and cape, and rushed from her mother's rooms.

The princess' last stop was the tanner. The low, open structure was located far from the palace, and anyone else, because of the stench. This made it very easy to find. Kandake wove her way round the vats and troughs of soaking skins. At the very back of the building, she heard Nuri's long blade scraping across rawhide and headed in that direction.

Walking through the workroom, the princess passed hides stretched on frames in various stages of the curing process. Vats of soaking animal skins stood against the wall. Blades for cutting and scraping dangled from a rack in front of the tanner. Kandake ducked around them and waited to be acknowledged. The rank air forced her to breathe through her mouth, panting lightly, but courtesy forbade her to complain.

Nuri laid her blade aside and unfolded her long body from the stool upon which she sat. She came from behind the table and dipped to one knee in respect while brushing bits of putrid flesh from her arms.

"Uncle Dakká said for me to pick up a package from you," Kandake said, acknowledging the woman's show of respect.

Standing, Nuri took a long, measuring look at the young princess as she pulled something from the shelf above Kandake's head.

"Prince Dakká had me make this for you weeks ago." She handed Kandake the package. "He instructed me to hold onto this until you came for it."

Kandake hefted the parcel before unwrapping it. Raising it to her face, she caught the tangy aroma of cured animal skin. With care, she pulled away the covering, revealing a sculpture of leather that appeared to be a body-double for her.

"A warrior queen requires her own breastplate," Nuri said. "It is made of several layers of hides bound together for protection from arrows and knives. It is dyed and polished to match your skin." She took it from Kandake's hands, turning it over to reveal the inside. "This portion is left without polish. It will wick away moisture and treat your skin to a gentle caress, no matter how long you wear it. But it must be washed when you bathe to prevent any irritation."

With eagerness, Kandake removed her bow and slipped the quiver of arrows from her back. Nuri placed the breastplate in position. It lifted the breasts and held them snug up against the body. Two leather straps began at the shoulders and crossed in the back. They passed through the center of another molded square of the heavy plate material that stretched around to meet the front side. It protected her back and had extra reinforcement over her spine. "In case some coward tries to put an arrow into your back," Nuri said.

With the breastplate in place, Kandake gazed down at her form. Running her hands over the surface brought the sensation of smooth skin. She turned this way and then that, testing it for freedom of movement. It neither hindered, rubbed, nor pinched—moving with her in fluid motion.

"This is beautiful." Kandake ran her hand over the smooth leather again. "The fit is perfect. How do I thank you for something as lovely as this?"

"There is no thanks needed, Princess Kandake," the tanner said. "It is my desire to see to the safety of our future queen."

Bow and arrows arranged appropriately, she made small adjustments to her sling and knife. Kandake whipped her travel cape around her shoulders, tying it at her neck. She bowed her appreciation to Nuri and left to meet her uncle at the caravan.

Powerful strides took her through the community. She allowed her ankle bells to sing, announcing the presence of Nubia's warrior queen.

11

Kandake walked toward the meeting place from which the caravan was to leave. Three oxen-drawn wagons stood loaded and waiting for final instructions. Ezena ran to meet her.

"You mean the king finally let you go on escort?" Ezena said. "I was worried that you would never get the chance."

"Me, too," Kandake said. "If it had not been for Uncle Dakká, I might still be waiting. I am really glad we get to go out together."

"Ooh, what is this?" Ezena ran her hand down the side of Kandake's new breastplate.

"It is beautiful. Uncle Dakká had it made for me. He said that it is what every warrior queen needs." She touched the bracelet circling her friend's wrist. "What is this?"

"Nateka made this for me."

"Now he is making you jewelry and you are wearing it. It looks like you have made up your mind about him. This relationship could get in the way of your warrior training."

"So could your training to become queen. You are not letting that stop you. Why should this stop me? I really like him, but it is too soon to make my mind up about anything."

Uncle Dakká signaled for everyone to get mounted.

Kandake walked to the other side of the second wagon where a servant waited for her, holding the reins of her horse. From withers to hoof, the animal stood fifteen hands tall. Wide spaced intelligent eyes watched her as she approached. His dark bay coat had been brushed to a high gloss. He raised his well-groomed tail and bobbed his head.

"Strong Shadow," Kandake called his name and whistled. He stamped his feet in anticipation. Accepting the leather leads, she vaulted to his back, whispering soothing encouragement into his ear and brought him to stand next to Ezena's mount.

"Princess Kandake," Uncle Dakká said, riding up to the two girls. "You will be riding next to me. We will stay together throughout the journey."

Kandake nodded her understanding, then said, "Thank you for this wonderful gift." She stroked the breastplate with a loving caress. "It is beautiful."

"You are very welcome. A warrior queen needs her protection." He winked then signaled for those leading the caravan to start.

An apprentice, paired with a seasoned warrior, trotted ahead to scout the route. From the way the muscles rippled in the apprentice's back and the manner he sat his mount, Kandake recognized her friend and sparring partner, Amhara.

On the opposite side of the wagon, Kandake glimpsed Ezena observing her watching the young man's back.

"My cousin sits his horse well, does not he?" Ezena teased.

"You and I will begin here next to the second wagon," Uncle Dakká said, drawing his niece's attention. "Open your eyes and your mind to everything around you. I expect that bandits will be watching soon enough."

A thrill of excitement coursed through her. She pulled a thin leather thong from Strong Shadow's pack and tied her braids into place at the base of her neck. The cape she wore trailed out behind her, reaching to the rump of her horse. Sitting tall on Strong Shadow's back, Kandake eyed the terrain surrounding them for any sign of the bandits.

I dare you. Show yourself, she challenged, half-hoping something would arise from behind a bush. *If you do, you will meet the point of a well-aimed arrow.*

Kandake laughed at herself. She sounded as war hungry as Tabiry accused her of being.

"Notice how the center of the road is full of wagon tracks, ruts, and deep hoof prints," Uncle Dakká said, after the caravan had traveled some distance from the kingdom. "It is meant for us to believe that only our caravans, and others like them, travel here. Look closely at the short grasses beside the road."

Kandake studied where he indicated. Hidden among the light weeds, she spotted imprints of horses' hooves. They were deep, indicating they carried riders. She counted about fifteen. Her hand went to her bow.

"You have missed something," her uncle said. Reaching with his hand, he prevented her drawing the weapon. "See how there are no sharp edges to the prints. Did you notice that the grass is standing through them? These riders are not close by. They passed through here some time ago. The scouts will tell us how long."

Uncle Dakká turned to face her. "It is the same as when tracking an animal in the hunt. Use those same skills here."

Kandake compared the tracks at the side of the road with those made by the wagon and riders ahead of her. She could see the sharpness of their marks and the grasses they rode over continued to lie down. The tracks beside the road had grass and stubble poking through them. There was a lot for her to learn and she planned to take it all in.

She paid close attention to what her uncle taught her as they rode together. He pointed out important features of the landscape, like where to expect an ambush on turns of the road or how to tell if an enemy was hiding beneath the sand.

"Look for an abrupt end in the grass-line," he said. "Where one lies beneath the sand, nothing grows." He questioned her on the different tracks they encountered, the importance of the direction of the wind to an arrow's flight, and the scents the air current carried to them, noting the difference between animal and man.

Not long after the scouts returned with their report, Uncle Dakká ordered camp for the night. Because there had been no report of danger, a fire was lit and a travel stew prepared. Kandake served her uncle and sat next to him with her own dinner. She took pleasure in the open view of the night sky and marked each star for their direction in relation to her home. She listened to the creatures scuttling along in the darkness. Filling her mouth, she chewed on each savory bit with delight.

Kandake and Uncle Dakká enjoyed a relaxing conversation with their meal. They talked about her friends, old pets she used to have, and hunting trips they had shared. Before long, Amhara and Ezena joined them. Uncle Dakká excused himself to meet with the seasoned warriors.

"What do you think they are talking about?" Kandake asked her friends.

"Probably the bandits Kashta and I tracked," Amhara told her. "We followed their trail for a long way along this route."

"Do you think they will attack?" The question bubbled out of Kandake in a mixture of fear and excitement.

"He does not think so. At least, not until we have gotten beyond Egypt."

"Why wait until then?" Ezena wondered. "We are carrying a valuable load now."

"Kashta thinks they will wait until we have traded and are heavy with new woods. Loaded like that and being pulled by oxen, we could not outrun them," Amhara said, then fell silent.

"I think I know what they are waiting for," Kandake interjected into the quiet. "The bandits are waiting to follow us to the frankincense groves. Then they would get a double prize, rob us, take the groves, and send us running back to the kingdom. Too bad for them, Nubian warriors never run."

12

Several days of travel and trade proved to make good profit and the caravan made for the frankincense groves. Spirits were light. Tradesmen brought out musical instruments to accompany those singing. But Uncle Dakká and the experienced warriors were on alert. Kandake watched the movement of her uncle's eyes. They scoured the countryside. So many days of riding left her body achy, making it difficult for her to remain watchful.

Kashta and Amhara rode in front of the caravan. They were followed by two wagons filled with fresh timber. It would be cured and hardened for future benches, tables, and other pieces of furniture. And because trade had gone so well, they were able to acquire two wagonsful to their usual one. Casks of precious and semiprecious stones lay hidden beneath the wood.

On either side of the second wagon rode a warrior and apprentice pair, Kurru and Ezena on one side and Senka and Nedjeh on the other. Uncle Dakká and Kandake brought up the rear behind the third wagon.

"Uncle, we should be taking the left fork," Kandake said. He silenced her with a hand signal. Her brisk nod told him she understood. His gaze darting to the left indicated the direction of danger. Further gestures told her to drop her reins and steer Strong Shadow with her knees. Up ahead, she could see the other warriors doing the same. They rode on, prepared for the imminent attack.

The lead wagon of the caravan passed through a narrow opening into a shallow basin of dying trees and over-grown vegetation. These no longer produced the fragrant sap, but it was enough to fool the bandits into showing their hand. The last wagon came through the opening and trundled to a stop, partially blocking the entrance. The other two wagons nestled themselves among the trees, making it difficult for anyone access to their cargo.

Several of the tradesmen climbed down from their perches and pretended to begin harvesting the trees. As if this were their cue, the bandits poured into the gorge, but the placement of the third wagon slowed them down.

The warriors whirled to meet them, bows in hand, arrows nocked. Screeching like wild animals, the bandits bore down on them, attempting to encircle the caravan.

"Follow me," Uncle Dakká commanded Kandake. "Do exactly as I do." He let his first arrow fly and kicked his mount into motion. She urged Strong Shadow to pursue and let go her first flight. Weaving in and out of the trees, the company of warriors met their attackers.

Eight more had joined the fifteen bandits that Kashta and Amhara trailed. This placed the warriors at a disadvantage of nearly three to one. The bandits were good on horseback. They were good with the bow, but not as good as Nubian warriors.

Kandake laced between and around the dying trunks following her uncle. Her shots were good, but her uncle's were deadly. On several passes through the trees, she crossed in front of Amhara or behind Ezena. Her focus split between following Uncle Dakká and keeping track of the bandits' positions.

Her arms grew weary. Her fingers felt tender. But the bandits continued to come. Strong Shadow blew and snorted his tired determination to keep going as long as she drove him forward. Dust filled the air, kicked up by so many horses running and turning in the confined space. Kandake felt the weight of the sand that clung to her uncovered, sweat-drenched skin.

A few of the attackers abandoned their horses and went for the wagons. From the corner of her eye, she saw Kashta and Amhara dismount mid-gallop to give chase. When they reached them, Amhara pulled one bandit from behind. Kashta blocked the knife thrust of the one that turned to face him. The four fought hand-and-knife.

Soon there were fewer bandits than there were warriors. In what seemed like desperation and fearing the Nubian archers, the bandits took the fight to the ground, as if hoping to gain the advantage. Kurru and Senka had been injured. The remaining six warriors fought in even combat with the last of the bandits.

The man wrestling with Kandake was no taller than she, but he weighed twice as much. Seeing that she was female, he taunted her. Hurling insults and jibes, he dared her to come at him.

Her first blows knocked him backward, but nothing more than that. He slammed his fist into the side of her head. Her ears rung and stars burst into her sight. Her knees buckled, owing to her loss of equilibrium. She staggered against a wagon. Then he was on top of her. He wrapped his arms about Kandake to crush her.

"I am going to snap you like a sapling." He breathed into her ear, squeezing tighter and tighter, his ugly grin inches from her nose as the edges of her vision began to darken.

She snaked her arm across her belly and between her body and the attacker's. Kandake reached around far enough to get hold of her knife. She eased it from its sheath, pulling it back across with stealth between their bodies. She thrust the blade just around his side and upward into his back. Tugging the blade out made a smacking sound and his warm blood oozed over her hand.

Kandake watched his grin falter. A querying look came into his eyes as his grip loosened.

Her attacker fell away from her. With him on the ground, Kandake's lungs were free to expand. She dragged air into them. Then, as if slammed in her middle, her stomach forced its contents up, straining to get out. Doubled over, she retched and spewed until her belly was beyond empty.

Kandake straightened and brought a trembling hand to wipe her mouth. But the shaking did not stop at her hand. It traveled the length of her arm and covered her entire body, shuddering from a concoction of fear, fatigue, and rage. Just as she found her calm, Amhara slammed into her side. The force sent her to the ground.

Climbing to her feet, she reached for him to gain her balance. Amhara collapsed under the pressure. He fell against her with an arrow protruding from his side. Kandake eased him to the ground and turned to follow the line of flight the arrow had taken. The remaining bandit stood near the entrance to the basin. He faced her and lowered his bow. Their eyes met. A cruel grin slithered over his face.

Rage infused her. Snatching her sling from her hip, Kandake galloped across the distance, intent on wiping his face clean of all expression. Her eyes never left that man. He turned to run. She filled her sling. He pumped his legs. She twirled her sling. He ran. She ran faster. At full tilt Kandake hurled the stone. It caught him at the base of his skull as he entered the pass, bringing him down.

Satisfied he would never rise, Kandake returned to her friend.

13

"Is he all right?" Kandake asked those surrounding Amhara. Her friend was sitting on the ground with his back resting against the wheel of a wagon. The blood that had been pouring from his side had slowed to a trickle. He managed a weak smile as she came nearer.

"It is a bad wound," her uncle said, completing his examination of the wounded apprentice. "We should get him back before it festers." He used a bit of cloth to wipe the blood from his hands.

"What about the groves?" Kandake looked to the tradesmen. Seeing their discouraged faces, she turned back to her uncle. "We need this harvest. I doubt there is enough frankincense to make incense for trade or kohl for the Egyptians. And I know that we need a load to keep the supply of medicine at its best. We cannot possibly go back without it."

"Kurru has a broken leg and the gash on Senka's head is pretty deep." Uncle Dakká stared off into the trees as if considering the possible options available to him. "No." He turned to his niece. "We have to return without going to the groves."

"Uncle, we have to go. This is the last harvest of the season before the monsoons start. Once they begin, we will not be able to get back here."

"It cannot be helped."

"Then we split up. You go on ahead with the caravan. I will go to the groves and harvest what I can. Afterward, I will meet up with you before you reach Nubia."

"I will not allow you to go there by yourself. I told your father I would keep you with me."

"Then you can go to the groves with me. I am not going back without that harvest."

"Kandake, do not push me on this." Uncle Dakká's face was stone. "You can see the dangers, you are not a child." He stood in front of her. The veins pulsing in his neck mimicking the appearance of chords of rope gave evidence to his rising temper.

"You are right, Uncle." Kandake held her ground, her anger matching his. "I am not a child. I am a woman and successor to the throne of Nubia. My first duty is to see to the needs of those who depend on me." She faced him, matching his stance of determination and presented herself as an immovable force. There they stood as figures cast from hard metal, eyes locked, wills of iron.

"Prince Dakká." Kashta insinuated himself between them, careful to give neither the offense of his back. "I believe there is a solution that will please you both, if you will allow me?" He squatted on the ground and outlined his plan in the dirt. Kandake and Uncle Dakká hunkered down with him, forcing them to abandon their battle positions.

"What if we divide the caravan?" Kashta stalled Uncle Dakká's protest with an uplifted hand. "The two full wagons and our wounded begin the trek back to Nubia, and the third goes to the groves with you and Princess Kandake. Both needs would be met."

"The caravan would be defenseless," Uncle Dakká said.

"Weakened, but not defenseless. Kurru only has a broken leg; his bow arm is still good. Nedjeh will remain with me. He and I can alternate scouting for our safe passage. Senka cannot ride, but his bow is threatening enough.

"That leaves Ezena to go with the two of you. Surely three Nubian warriors can protect one wagon."

"He is right, Uncle." Kandake's enthusiasm for the plan swept away the remains of her anger. "If we use horses instead of oxen we can move faster."

In the end, Kandake and Kashta got Uncle Dakká to agree to split the caravan. They harnessed the riderless mounts to the wagon. Though horses could not pull as much weight as oxen, they would not need to. The frankincense would be lighter to carry and the speed of the horses would get them to and from the groves in less than half the time. Several of the tradesmen joined them to help in the harvesting.

# # # #

"Do you smell that?" Kandake grinned at Ezena, filling her lungs with the spicy air. The small party entered the rocky gorge. Trees littered the ground, bursting into existence in a haphazard fashion. "I love it here among the trees."

"But will you be saying that by nightfall?" her friend reminded her, wagging a teasing finger. "By then the muscles in our backs will be burning from the constant bending and reaching, chipping away at the frankincense tears." The strands of dried sap that ran down the trees' trunks from gouges cut strategically in the bark.

"Do not leave out the aching hands and the blisters that our blisters will have," Kandake added, spirits high, but well aware of the hard work ahead.

As the wagon pulled into the farthest end of the grove, Kandake bounded from her perch and began unhitching the horses. She and Ezena fed and watered them. They tied them up nearby before joining the harvesters. Each took a sack and a chipping blade from the wagon and headed into the trees.

They worked long and hard. Work songs started up, taking everyone's minds off their tired muscles. By nightfall each had filled a collection sack, tied it off, and loaded it onto the wagon.

Throughout the day, Kandake caught glimpses of Uncle Dakká as he made a wide scouting circle of the grove on horseback. When he returned, her uncle pronounced it safe to light a fire. He brought with him small animals he hunted while checking the perimeter. The cooks cleaned the carcasses and added them to the pot for their meal.

"Do you think Amhara will be all right?" Kandake asked Ezena. They sat resting their backs against a tree with their bowls of stew. As hungry as she was, worry for her friend dulled her appetite.

"He should be fine once they get him back to Nubia," Ezena said through a mouthful. "Kashta does not think the arrow hit anything vital. The biggest worries are blood loss and fester."

"What was Amhara thinking? This breastplate would have stopped that arrow." She rapped her knuckles against the rigid, leather shell. "There was no need for him to put his life in danger like that."

"He was protecting his queen."

"I am not queen yet, not for a long time."

"You have always been his queen," Ezena said, eyes twinkling, "long before you were chosen for the throne."

14

Kandake watched her friend's smile match the twinkle in her eyes as the meaning of Ezena's words broke into her understanding.

"Are you saying what I think you are saying?" Kandake asked.

"It is not for me to tell. You will have to ask Amhara yourself."

"But you have to tell me...."

"Bank the fire for the night," Uncle Dakká ordered the party. "We harvest at first light. That means you, too." He directed his words toward his niece and her friend.

Kandake reached for Ezena's arm to press her point.

"As you wish, My Prince," Ezena said, evading Kandake's grasp with ease. Heading back toward the center of their camp, she threw a smile over her shoulder, teasing her friend.

# # # #

Kandake resented the sun's cheerful greeting, having had too little sleep the night before with her mind puzzling over Ezena's taunt about Amhara's name for her. She had no opportunity to question her friend. Uncle Dakká had set a frenzied work schedule for them all. He wanted to complete the harvest by early evening and use the last of the sun's light to begin the trek back to Nubia.

Her body slick with the sweat of hard labor, Kandake pushed on. Thoughts of Amhara's injury and what he had done distracted her.

He should have seen that the bandit's arrow shot from that distance was no match for this breastplate. What was he thinking? He should have been returning that man's arrow, not taking it.

Kandake's fury caused her to swing the tool with more force than she had intended, gouging the tree's bark. She realized her error and lightened her touch, then continued removing the tears of resin. It was a good thing this was a mature tree. It would heal over without damage.

She moved from tree to tree filling her sack and added it to the growing load in the wagon. Before she grabbed another bag, Kandake allowed herself a long drink of water, chewed a dried fig, and wiped away as much of the sweat as she could. With the heat near to unbearable, she reached for the release of the breastplate.

"I must insist that you keep that on, Princess," her uncle's firm voice directed. "We have no idea who may be watching. Your safety is paramount."

"But Uncle, I am melting away inside here."

"You are not taking it off. You have a duty to protect yourself."

"Yes, Uncle." She acquiesced only because it brought her mind back to Amhara and the reason for his actions.

I have a duty to protect myself and all of Nubia. That includes him. What was he thinking?

Kandake seethed as she returned to the backbreaking work of chipping away the dried pool of frankincense that formed at the base of the tree.

Throwing himself in front of that arrow, he could have been killed! Of all the dull-witted, half-cooked notions. When we catch up with the caravan, I am going to have something to say to that particular warrior.

Kandake reached up and wiped away the sweat from beneath her chin. She pulled a piece of cloth from her waist and mopped at the back of her neck. When she felt moisture dripping from her chin again, it occurred to her that she was crying.

The thought hit her that her friend could have been killed. He could be dying from his wound. She had killed two men and her friend could be dying. Hot tears coursed down her face. Anger mounted inside her.

All of this, over what? A few trees? Some jewels, and some pretty smelling sap that we are breaking our backs to chip off, bits at a time, under this blazing sun!

Kandake stood, stretched. She gazed at the men and women working in the grove with her. Their backs bent to the work, ignoring the agonizing waves of heat surrounding them. She thought of the families at home in Nubia who depended on this labor. She listed the benefits that would come from the profits of their trade. There would be more food, good medicine, and healthy livestock. These things ensured a good life to everyone she knew. Everyone these people knew.

So I will protect it. Every citizen of Nubia is worth it, every bit of it. You are right, Uncle, I have a duty to my kingdom Wearing this breastplate protects its future. And killing those that would rob Nubia protects its present.

_15_

The last of the sacks was piled into the wagon. Camp was cleared and the animals were gathered and harnessed.

"The horses are fresh," Uncle Dakká said. "Keep them at a steady trot. We will go as far as we can until we lose the daylight."

Kandake clambered onto the loaded wagon. Strong Shadow was hitched along with the other horses pulling it, adding his strength. Uncle Dakká scouted ahead and Ezena rode behind keeping an eye out for attackers. Weary bodies buoyed by light spirits enjoyed easy conversation, each taking his turn comparing blisters and strained muscles.

Kandake listened for a time, then allowed her mind to drift in and out of her own thoughts. Thoughts of returning to Nubia with full wagons and how that would add to the kingdom's wealth. Her mind slid to ideas of each item they brought back being worked by craftsmen and the goods they would produce. She thought about the lessons that would come out of their encounter with the bandits and preparations that would be made for the next caravan.

From there, her mind cruised to Amhara. How was he managing with his injury? She pulled her knees to her chin and recalled as much as she could about his wound.

The arrow had pierced his side from the back with the point protruding in the front. She had watched, fascinated, as the arrowhead was cut away. Then the wound was bathed with water to remove blood and dirt before the shaft was then pulled out.

Amhara had only hissed his pain. Uncle Dakká had instructed that the wound be slathered with a pungent paste whose base ingredient was frankincense. This would keep the wound clean and free from disease. Then they wrapped his midsection with strips of clean linen.

"Why had he put himself in danger like that?"

Kandake recalled Ezena's words. "He was protecting his queen."

What exactly does she mean, 'I was his queen before I was chosen for the throne'? Does she mean what I think she means? She let her mind drift to the many times they had sparred together. He had always acted in a way that said he liked her, but did that mean that he *liked* her? She examined every conversation she'd had with him that she could remember.

Amhara never acted the way Tabiry's suitors did. *Of course he would not act like that. Amhara is a strong, proud warrior, not some calf bawling for attention.*

Her musings led her to thinking of how Amhara handled himself in hand-to-hand practice with her. She pictured the way his powerful muscles rippled moving through stances and holds. Then there was the glistening of his rich, dark skin following an afternoon's workout. She could not forget his ready smile displaying his even, well-matched, white teeth.

"Kandake, did you hear what I said?" Ezena's insistent voice broke through her reverie. "Prince Dakká has signaled for you to guard behind the wagon."

Working to clear thoughts of Amhara from her mind, Kandake traded places with Ezena as the horse matched the speed of the wagon.

"Where was your mind?" her friend asked. "It would not be with my cousin, by any chance?"

Kandake dropped her eyes in embarrassment and rode to the rear of the wagon. Ezena's laughter followed her as she went.

Before long it became too dark to travel without risk. Uncle Dakká called the party to a halt.

"We will make camp here. Loose the horses, feed and water them," he directed. "No fire. I saw some tracks other than the caravan's. Tie the horses near the wagon."

"Do you think there are more bandits?" Kandake asked. She and Ezena exchanged a worried look.

"I am not sure, but we will not take any chances. Sleep lightly and keep your bows close. Kandake, get to sleep quickly," her uncle instructed. "I will wake you for your watch."

Kandake and Ezena unfolded their mats at the rear of the wagon. Kandake's uncle laid his out in front of it and took the first watch. The tension from the tradesmen was palpable. No one had much to say.

"Who does he think is out there?" Ezena asked, keeping her voice in a low whisper. "Bandits?"

"He says he does not know, but he is preparing just in case of an attack."

"I hope whoever it is does not come until light. Night drills were not my best."

Kandake smiled into the darkness. Her friend shot very nearly as well at night as she did in the daylight, both with lethal accuracy. Kandake placed her bow and arrows within easy reach. She rolled onto her side and drifted into a listening sleep.

The morning followed an uneventful night. Of the small party, only the horses appeared to be rested. Prancing their eagerness to get started, the animals repeated yesterday's pace with ease. This time Uncle Dakká remained close to the wagon. He instructed Kandake to keep watch with an arrow nocked from the top of the pile of filled sacks, while Ezena covered their rear.

By the end of the day they spotted the dust of the caravan not far beyond them. Uncle Dakká rode ahead to make contact with Kashta and check on his wounded. Before long the single wagon caught up to the other two. Halt was called and the horses were released from the wagon and replaced by oxen.

During the exchange, Kandake found an opportunity to check on Amhara. The wound had weakened him, but when his eyes met hers the strain on his face was exchanged for the smile she knew best.

"Amhara." Kandake spoke in a soothing, quiet voice while laying a gentle hand on his bandaged wound.

He sat a little straighter beneath her touch and whispered in response, "My queen."

_16_

After a day's ride, the caravan pulled into the courtyard of the palace. Nedjeh had ridden ahead to alert the court of their arrival and the caravan's need of a healer. King Amani and Nubia's chief healer met the wagons. A large group of servants began unloading the goods that had been obtained in trade.

"Where is she?" King Amani demanded. Worry covered his face. His eyes squinted against the lowering sun. "Nedjeh said the caravan was attacked."

"She is fine," Uncle Dakká answered his brother, ending his dismount in a bow before his king. "Your daughter has not been harmed."

"Then where is she?"

"Princess Kandake," Uncle Dakká said, projecting his voice past the wagons behind him. "The king wishes to see you."

Kandake swung down from Strong Shadow. She had been riding a protective position flanking the caravan. She approached her father with the dignity of a warrior. Kandake watched his eyes scrutinize her from head to foot and back up again. When she reached him, she lowered one knee to the ground, crossed her arms over her chest, and bowed her head, giving her father the respect of warrior to king. King Amani rested the palm of his hand on the back of Kandake's bowed head, a display of great favor from ruler to warrior.

Kandake's posture and demeanor exemplified the epitome of discipline and restraint. But inside she was bursting with excitement. She was dying to tell her father everything she had experienced. The travel, the trade, the hard labor, and the attack—all of it roiled inside of her, threatening to boil over.

"Stand, young warrior," King Amani commanded, but his voice belied the calm he portrayed. The moment Kandake rose to her feet King Amani pounced, smothering her within his tight embrace. "You are home, you are safe."

"I am home, I am safe." She repeated his words, feeling the security and shelter of them.

"Thank you, Prince Dakká," the king nodded to his brother. After the king was certain that his daughter was well and unharmed, he released the healer to check the injured warriors.

Kandake walked into the palace with her father. Even though nothing had changed since she had left, it was all different. Everything was more precious. It all held deeper meaning. The great hall greeted her with the warmth of things familiar. The images of past rulers engraved into the walls welcomed her. Their eyes questioned the depth of her commitment.

I know my duty, Great Ones, Kandake's heart assured them. *Nubia will be protected and safe with me*. Yet, she knew it went beyond duty for her. She felt a deep love for the kingdom and everyone in it.

Walking to where her mother worked and slept led them through corridors bearing images of Nubian caravans. Kandake walked a little taller. Her spine held arrow straight and shoulders squared evidenced her feelings of pride and purpose.

"My queen," King Amani said, entering his wife's rooms. "I bring you a most precious gift."

Kandake had been in this part of the palace many times, but it too was changed for her. The lengths of fabric covering the windows seemed more beautiful. Love and comfort permeated the air smelling of her mother, warmth and spice.

Queen Sake, seated on a silk covered bench, set aside the sheets of papyrus she had been studying. Kandake dropped to her knees beside her mother only to be enfolded in the queen's strong arms. She endured her mother's fawning, enjoying it more than she would have admitted. Finally, Queen Sake pushed her daughter away from her.

"This is not the child I presented to you," the queen accused her husband, jesting. "You have brought me a warrior. Where is my daughter?"

"I am here," Kandake chuckled, "beneath all of this." She removed her bow with its quiver of arrows and stripped away the breastplate. Untying the sling and knife from her hips, Kandake placed it all on the bench next to her mother.

A servant entered the room, gathered Kandake's things from the bench, and put them away. She offered

Kandake a cool, refreshing drink of her favorite, pomegranate juice.

"Mother, it was exciting and terrifying all at the same time." She wiped the dribble of juice from her chin with the back of her hand. "I have to tell you everything."

"Princess," her father admonished. "Your duty is to report to the council first. It convenes as soon as you have bathed and dressed." King Amani bent to kiss his wife then whispered in a voice that carried to Kandake. "Sake, I promise I will send her the moment we end."

Kandake watched her father's words soften the look of irritable disappointment on her mother's face. "And I will run all the way." Kandake added her promise to his.

# # # #

The council convened in the chamber off the throne room. At the meeting room's center stood the table bearing the stone inlay of the map of Nubia. Maps of the surrounding area covered the walls. At the table, Kandake sat next to King Amani. His siblings in attendance made up the members of the kingdom's council. Next to them sat Kandake's brothers and sister. Each of King Amani's children joined the meeting as they would be the next ruler and council members for the coming generation. Behind Kandake sat two scribes to take notes on the council proceedings.

Servants placed burnished gold vessels filled with a refreshing mixture of fruit juices in front of each attendee. Against the far wall stood a long narrow table, its top covered with platters of food. Each one piled with wedges of fruit, thick slices of pork and lamb, or fresh rounds of radishes and onion in alternating layers of blocks of cheese. At either end of the tabletop set pitchers of fruit juice and water. Servants stood waiting to provide refreshment throughout the length of this meeting.

"Prince Dakká," King Amani opened the meeting. "How are our warriors faring?"

Uncle Dakká nodded to Kashta, giving him permission to report to the king.

"Senka's head is mending well. The healer says that he will be able to resume his duties within a few days. Kurru's leg will heal straight, but that will take several weeks."

"And what of the apprentice?" the king asked. "How bad are his injuries?"

Kandake's ears pricked up, listening as Kashta gave an account of Amhara's progress. She cared about the other warriors, but Amhara was different. He had to be all right. After all, it was her fault that he was injured in the first place.

I still cannot believe he stepped in front of that arrow. I keep asking myself why. Ezena's explanation? He really cares for me like that? Oh please, let him be all right.

"The healer reports that Amhara will recover," Kashta continued. "It will take several weeks for his side to heal. After that, once he rebuilds his strength he will return to training."

Kandake felt her body relax as she released a long, slow breath. Her uncle gave the formal report on the attack of the caravan. He spoke of how they were trailed and the way they had led the bandits into one of the abandoned groves. Uncle Dakká praised the skills of his warriors, particularly the apprentices.

"They kept their heads," he said. "Their training won out over whatever fears or feelings they may have had."

He described for his brother Kandake's prowess in her first dangerous confrontation that led to the deaths of two of the bandits.

Kandake watched her father's expression flow from fear to anger to triumphant pride as her uncle did the telling. When the account came to an end, everyone in the room turned faces filled with praise and approval on Kandake. Everyone, that is, except Tabiry.

The scribes chronicled Uncle Dakká's report in its entirety. They maintained scrupulous accounts of all points and conversation taking place within the council as it would become a permanent part of Nubia's history

Then those at the table turned their attention to Prince Naqa. He gave an accounting of the trades that were made and the goods Nubia had obtained. King Amani nodded and grunted at the gains for their kingdom. The extra timber and gemstones meant more items for trade, creating greater profit for the next trade season. The major part of the frankincense they harvested would replenish their supply of medicine. The rest of it would be employed to make incense and kohl, to be used by Nubians and for trade.

"In all, Nubia is again assured to maintain its position of wealth," Uncle Naqa said, coming to the end of his account.

The king thanked him for his report, and then turned to Uncle Dakká. "What can you tell me about the bandits that attacked the caravan?"

"Not much, My King. We searched their clothing for clues of their origin, but each robed himself in a different manner."

"Prince Dakká, if I may?" Kashta interjected. At the prince's permission, he continued. "After you and the princess left us to harvest frankincense, I had Nedjeh loose one of their horses and follow it to see which bearing it would take.

"It headed in the general direction of Assyria. We cannot make the assumption that the bandits came from there, but…."

"You think Assyria sent them to attack our caravan?" Uncle Dakká asked, skeptical. "What would they gain?"

"I do not think they sent them," Kashta said. "But it does point to their supplying them. If not that, they have at the least given them a place of refuge. Why else would the horse return to them?"

Kandake panned the faces of those around the table. Everyone appeared to be deep in thought. Her father's brow creased in concern. Something troubled him, but what? She waited for one of her elders to speak into the silence.

"My King," Aunt Alodia's voice was made louder by the quiet. "We must consider Egypt's request. The implications of these bandits tied, however loosely, to

Assyria requires serious examination. Unless we exercise wisdom, war will come to Nubia."

Kandake examined the countenance of each council member and her siblings, looking for hints of Aunt Alodia's meaning. When her gaze landed on Tabiry, what it took in were eyes smoldering with fury, directed at her.

17

Several hours and one very long, unresolved discussion later, Kandake returned to her mother's rooms. She found her giving orders to servants regarding the restocking of palace supplies. Kandake used her waiting time to digest the meaning of the council's discussion.

Could war really come here? And if we supply Egypt with archers to help them against Assyria, where would that leave Nubia?

All I have are questions. What I need are answers.

"Kandake?" her mother called from across the room. "What has got your faced tied up in knots?"

"I was thinking about the council meeting. Father has some really difficult decisions to make."

"Ruling is filled with difficult decisions. He will choose what is best for the kingdom. The council and your Aunt Alodia help him use sound judgment."

Queen Sake dismissed the remaining servant and sat on the bench next to her daughter. "Will you tell me about the caravan?" She plucked a few nuts from a nearby dish and popped them into her mouth.

It took a moment for Kandake to quell the heaviness of the council meeting and regain the excitement of the journey. With sights and sounds placed in her mind, she began her tale.

"Waset was beautiful. It was busy with people moving from place to place, full of their day's business. I could see everywhere bits of our trade and craft—morsels of Nubia living among the Egyptians." She snagged a savory olive. Sliding it into her cheek she held it there, sucking the brine, and resumed her tale.

"In the marketplace," Kandake said, her voice pitched higher with excitement, "our goods were preferred. They favored our kohl and medicines over their own. Everywhere we went it was the same. Two stops beyond Egypt all of our wares were exchanged. Our wagons were heavier with payment than they were with the goods we took to trade."

"Now tell me about the journey," her mother said, reflecting Kandake's zeal. She waved a servant into the room to bring them liquid refreshment. "How was it? Did you learn anything new?"

"Uncle Dakká taught me how to read different types of signs. How to tell the age of a trace and count the number in their party. It is similar to tracking animals for the hunt, but there are fewer animal droppings to give hints. He also taught me how to judge where an ambush is sure to be set along a route.

"Did he teach you how to kill?" Tabiry said, entering the room. "It seems you have learned that lesson very well."

Kandake met her sister's accusing glare without wavering. While she found no pleasure in taking the life of another, she felt no shame in protecting those in her care. She rose from her seat, meeting her sister on even ground.

"I did what had to be done, Tabiry," Kandake told her. "A warrior's duty is to protect those she is charged to safeguard."

"But that is not what happened, is it?" Tabiry stood nose-to-nose with her sister, wagging an accusing finger. "Amhara was wounded protecting you. He almost died. And the man you brought down with a sling-stone, he was on his way out of the gorge. How could he have been a threat to you or anyone else?"

"That is what you do not understand." Kandake lowered her voice and slowed her speech as if she were instructing a simple child. "If that man had left, he could have gone for help. We had no way of knowing how many he would bring back with him and there were only a precious few of us, counting the three that were injured."

"You could have captured him, questioned him about the others. You did not have to kill him. You and Natasen will bring war to this kingdom just to satisfy your need to be strong." Tabiry's eyes were overflowing, sending angry tears down her cheeks. "You and your warrior ways will destroy Nubia."

Queen Sake moved to intervene between her daughters. Kandake held her hand up halting her mother's progress without taking her eyes from her sister.

Standing as tall as the young woman facing her, Kandake placed her hands on Tabiry's shoulders, giving them a gentle squeeze. "I love Nubia as much as you, if not more. I do not want war here anymore than you do. What you have to understand is that if war comes, Nubia must be strong. All of us."

Kandake led her sister to a longer bench and invited her mother to join them. "Let me tell you everything that happened during that attack," Kandake began once they were seated. "There was no doubt of our danger."

She explained to them how Uncle Dakká had identified they were being followed and used the caravan to lead the bandits to the field of dead trees. Kandake walked through the telling with great detail. She recounted the attack and counter-attack that occurred in the basin.

When she got to the part about the bandit having her in his death grip, her breath caught. She scrubbed her face with her hands and pushed on.

"His arms were like knotted cords of iron. No matter how I kicked or twisted, I could not loosen them enough to suck in air." Her voice was hoarse. Her eyes stared at the scene visible only to her. Tears dripped from her chin.

"It was the middle of the day, but light dimmed like the sun was setting, sliding away into the night. But that could not be, it was only late morning. It could only mean that I was dying." Kandake pulled in a deep breath and let it out with a long shudder.

"I felt death nearby. I did not want to die. I managed to wriggle my arm between our bodies and grabbed hold of my knife. With his foul breath he hissed about breaking me like a young tree. I shoved my blade into his back." Bile rose to the back of her throat. She swallowed. Then swallowed again, forcing the bitter liquid to return to its proper place.

"I felt his hot blood bubble over my hand. I watched life's light leaving his eyes. Then, I could breathe again and he was lying at my feet." Kandake loosed another shuddering breath. Deflated and devoid of energy she forced herself to continue.

"I was cleaning the last of the bandit's blood from my knife when Amhara slammed into me, knocking me over. I pulled on his arm as he helped me to stand. He fell to his knees. That is when I saw the arrow jutting from his side."

Kandake reached for the drinking vessel sitting in front of her. Her hand trembled. She snatched it back, then wiped it on her linen-covered thigh and reached again. This time it was as steady as the moon sliding through the night sky.

Lifting the vessel, Kandake sucked at its contents, emptying it. She set it back on the low table in front of her. Nodding her head, she encouraged herself to finish what she had started.

"I was furious. These bandits had prepared to attack a defenseless caravan. Even though we were there, they outnumbered us. They were not trying to rob us. They wanted to kill us. And this one was free and away. Instead of leaving, he turned to take a final life. And I took his instead.

"I will not allow my people to be hunted, to be plucked like geese. You worry that I will bring war to

Nubia. It could find us without my help." She stood to face her mother and sister.

"I do not need someone's death to tell me that I am strong. I am a Nubian warrior. I am strength. I will use that strength to protect this kingdom. Each of her citizens is my responsibility and that is worth my life."

18

Kandake lay in her bed, but she could not sleep. Recounting the events of the attack had her mind chasing question after question. Would Nubia be able to remain at peace? Would she get dragged into the war of her neighbor? What was best for this kingdom?

Abandoning any hope of sleep, she threw the light coverings from her legs. Sliding a lightweight tunic over her head, Kandake walked through the palace to the rear courtyard.

The night air was cool and refreshing. The stars overhead sparkled, winking as if they alone knew the secrets of the future. In the distance, sounds of animals moving through the darkness reached her ears. The quiet movements changed to the distant screeches of hunter and prey. The air carried the mixed aromas of meals cooked late, the droppings of healthy cattle, and the fragrance of incense laced with frankincense and other spices.

"I am not the only one having trouble sleeping," Alara said to Kandake as she approached the pillar he leaned against. He pulled the chewing stick from his mouth. He had used it to clean his teeth, but his long habit of sucking on the fragrant stem had kept it in his mouth. "Aunt Alodia has my brain going in circles. Which is the position of wisdom? Send Egypt archers as they request? Retain them in case Assyria is planning to assault Nubia? Should the king question Assyria about their sheltering the bandits that attacked our caravans? It is all too much." He held his head as if to prevent it from flying apart.

Kandake slid her back down the column and sat on the cool stones near where Alara stood. She drew her knees beneath her chin and stared out into the night.

"At least you do not have the deaths of two men chasing sleep away from you. Or a sister that declares that you will destroy Nubia all by yourself." Fatigue squeezed her voice until it croaked.

"Tabiry allows her fears to tell her what to think. I spoke with Uncle Dakká about those men. He said there was no other choice. It was a good decision, the only option you had. You have nothing to be ashamed of." He sat down on the stones next to Kandake. "As queen, you will have to make choices that nobody else likes. Our father is faced with that right now. Aunt Alodia can only advise him, but he is the one who chooses."

"But how do I know that the choice I make is right? At the time, killing those men seemed like the only thing I could do."

"What about now? Would you change what you did?"

"I do not think so. Those men may have had families—people depending on them. And because of me, they will never see them again."

Alara slid closer to his sister. He draped his arm across her shoulders and pulled her to himself. "I cannot know how you feel. I have only killed meat for our tables. But I know that if those men had not chosen to be bandits, had not chosen to attack our caravan, they would not have been there for you to fight."

Kandake laid her head on her brother. His warmth was comforting. His words were a balm to her spirit. The darkness of the night enfolded her in its blanket. Beginning to relax, she felt herself drift into a light doze.

"What is this I hear about you being Amhara's queen?"

Kandake jumped. Alara's voice startled her as much as the question did.

She stalled, giving herself time to think before she answered him. *What should I say? I do not know any more than you do. Amhara is strong and I guess he is handsome. In all of the time we have spent together, sparring, I have never thought of him beyond that.*

"Do you think of him in that way?" Alara asked, breaking into her thoughts. "As a suitor?"

"I do not know. I have always enjoyed his company, I just never thought of him as someone I might take as a husband."

"Then I should tell him to change his thoughts about you," her brother remarked in mock sternness.

He made as if he were getting up to handle the problem.

"No! That is not what I am saying." Kandake pulled at his arm preventing him from leaving.

"So you do like him?"

"I have always liked him." She batted at Alara's playful, teasing gestures. "I just never gave much thought to marrying anyone. The flattering kittens that surround Tabiry are sickening. There is nothing about that that is appealing. My plans have always been filled with developing my skills as a warrior and building my strength. But Amhara is different." She flicked away a beetle that was trundling in a straight line for her toes. "I guess if I wanted a husband it would be someone like him. If he presented himself as a suitor, I do not believe I would object."

A huge yawn punctuated her statement. The tension had released its grip on her heart and mind, leaving her feeling sleepy and ready for bed. Kandake wished her brother a good night and returned to her rooms.

Sliding between the light coverings was a welcome refuge from the worries that had plagued her. Talking with Alara always soothed Kandake. Only on rare occasions did he give her the answers she needed, but talking with him allowed her mind room to navigate to a satisfactory conclusion.

It is curious how some people respond to fear. Alara is right. Tabiry lets hers create something to worry about. She is afraid that war might come to Nubia. She blames anyone she can for the possibility.

Father and the council are just as afraid, but they are looking for ways to prevent it.

Kandake rolled from her back onto her side. Her mind shifted to another subject. A more pleasant one, but just as puzzling—Amhara.

I am sure the healer would allow a short visit. Maybe even to sit in the garden? She felt her face pull into a smile. *I do like him.*

19

Several weeks after her return from the caravan, Kandake was enjoying what had become a regular schedule of visits with Amhara. They sat together in a shaded corner of the small garden at the back of the healer's residence. As they finished the last of their shared mid-day meal, Kandake watched Amhara stretch his healing side.

"How is it feeling today?" she asked.

"Much looser," Amhara answered, his voice breathy from the effort. "The healer thinks that I can begin light sparring." He leaned to the left, reaching beyond his head, plucking imaginary fruit from the air. His skin glistened in the afternoon sun. Kandake watched the rippling of his muscles.

He is nothing like those silly drones that follow my sister around. Wherever she goes, there they are, fawning over her. Flattering everything she does. Hanging on every word she says as if she held the wisdom of the world. Amhara is a warrior, strength carved into every line.

Amhara talked through his stretch. His every movement held Kandake's attention, but she heard little of what he said.

"Kashta has me working the beginning strength exercises again. Ezena has promised to come and work with me later."

"Uh-huh," she responded. The extension and flexing of his arms and side brought back thoughts of the attack.

"Are you listening?" Amhara finished his stretches. He mopped his face with a piece of cotton cloth and joined her on the bench.

Shaking herself, Kandake returned to the conversation. "Mm. Answer a question for me. Why do you think those bandits attacked the way they did?"

"What do you mean?" Amhara stopped mopping and turned to face her.

"I mean, they were not trying to rob us. It was more like they were trying to kill us. Or, at the least, prove our skill. Think about it." She was up and pacing. The movement helped her mind work through the puzzle that had been gnawing at her since their return.

"Look back over the attack. Not one of them tried to take the wagons. Instead they came at us with force." She saw Amhara's brow furrow with concentration. He pulled at his lower lip. When he nodded his head, indicating that his thoughts had caught up with hers, she continued.

"And their clothes. They added odd bits to their dress to make us think they came from a specific region. Regular bandits would not do that."

"I see what you mean. Bandits would have made sure there were not any clues to tell where to find them."

"Why did they?"

"Why did who do what?" Ezena asked, entering the garden.

"Why did the bandits wear clues to where they came from," Amhara answered her.

"That is the question that is traveling throughout the warriors' quarters," Ezena added, joining them. "There is something going on in the neighboring kingdoms and we appear to be right in the middle of it."

"Any one of them would love to get their hands on our lands." Kandake scowled. "There is no way I am going to let that happen, even if I have to fight them off by myself."

"You are not the only one who feels that way," Amhara assured her, standing and flexing his wounded side. His fingers kneaded the stiff muscles.

"He is right." Ezena said. "Every warrior in Nubia is ready to protect our home with their last breath. Prince Dakká has ordered that all of us are to prepare ourselves. Be ready.

"And that includes you, too," she said, turning toward Amhara. She examined her cousin's side. "If you are not careful, this coddling will make you soft." She gave him a playful nudge.

"Not if Kashta has anything to do with it. He has my schedule laid out for me." He made slow circles with his head, loosening his neck before returning to the bench. "Stretches in the morning and sparring in the afternoon. He even has a hunt planned for me."

"That sounds like the Prince's doing. Maybe he thinks he can sweat certain thoughts out of you," Ezena teased, glancing toward Kandake.

Kandake froze. She felt a little embarrassed, but stole a quick look in Amhara's direction.

"I do not have that much sweat in me." He laughed, looking directly at Kandake.

20

The next few weeks were filled with council meetings in the mornings and training sessions with Uncle Dakká in the afternoon. Kandake used her evenings to relax as best she could. Sometimes she would hunt with her brothers or friends. Other times she would sit in her grandmother's rooms talking about past trades and the unique people that came through Nubia. Often, she shaped her choice of activity around avoiding Tabiry.

"Father still has not decided how he will respond to Egypt's request of archers," Kandake remarked to Alara on one of their evenings relaxing together. "What do you think he should do?"

"That is hard to say." Alara tossed a small stone into the water of the Nile where they sat cooling their feet. "If he chooses to help Egypt it could leave Nubia vulnerable to attack. And if he declines their request, Nubia could lose Egypt as a valuable ally, not to mention what we would lose in trade."

"It seems that no matter what he chooses, there will be a price for Nubia to pay." She turned toward the sounds of someone's approach. From a distance, with only the light of a quartered moon she could not see his face. But the lithe movement of his body and purposeful stride identified him as Amhara.

When he joined them, Amhara greeted Kandake's oldest brother and plopped himself down next to Kandake. "There is a large hunt scheduled for tomorrow. Are either of you going?"

"We cannot," Alara said. Disappointment tinged his voice. "We have a council meeting tomorrow that is likely to drag on through most of the day. Until things are settled, neither of us will be doing much hunting."

"I was hoping you would be going," Amhara said to Kandake. "I had planned to join your party. You track better than anyone."

"I am stuck here," she groaned. She was disappointed about missing the hunt, but what she regretted most was not getting to spend time with Amhara. "The council has serious concerns to consider and a decision has to be made."

The three sat in silence. Kandake wondered what she could say to Alara to get him to leave without teasing her about it.

"I have a few things to get done before the council meeting in the morning," Alara announced, rising to leave. "Do not stay out too late, little sister. Tomorrow's meeting promises to be long and grueling."

Kandake watched her brother walk away toward the palace. She was excited to be alone with Amhara. She felt different sitting here with him, something that changed the moment he sat down. A softness filled with warmth surrounded them.

"I had really looked forward to hunting with you," Amhara said, once her brother was gone. "Together we would have taken more game than anyone. With your tracking skills and both of our bows we would have been unbeatable."

"I wish I could go, too." Disappointment and longing colored her voice. "I love hunting. It is the only place we can use the skills we practice and see if we are getting it right."

"Kashta has been teaching me new tactics. One of them is how to be invisible in plain sight."

"If you are in plain sight, how can you be invisible?"

"Well," Amhara shifted his position, moving so that he was sitting closer to Kandake. He sat near enough that their bare arms did not quite touch, but the hairs on their skin tickled each other's. "First, you wrap your cape around you so that it reveals nothing more than your arms and legs, and those you keep covered with the sand or soil."

Kandake listened to his explanation of invisibility. Her mind hung on every word. She yearned for an opportunity to practice such skills, but she would not have the chance until she advanced in her skill level and Uncle Dakká said she was ready. For now, she reconciled herself to listening to Amhara. Not at all an unpleasant task.

His voice is strong like the rest of him. Kandake allowed her mind to drift as he spoke. *Now it is very hard to keep focused while we are sparring. Instead of feeling frustration when I cannot break his holds, I enjoy having his arms wrapped around me.*

Amhara had stopped talking. Kandake saw him watching her face and wondered if he had asked a question she had not heard, or worse, she had said what she had been thinking. She opened her mouth to tell him she had not heard him.

"No," Amhara said. "Let me speak." He rubbed the back of his neck. He dropped his hands to his sides and dug his fingers into the dirt he was sitting on, opening and closing on fistfuls of dust.

"I have feelings for you, Princess Kandake. Very strong feelings. I know you have not chosen to accept suitors, yet, but I want you to know that I will wait."

Kandake shifted uncomfortably beside him. The strong warrior she had trained with seemed filled with fear. She wanted to assure him that his words and intentions were welcome, but to rescue him in that fashion would bring him shame. It would be the same as saying he is weak. She sat in silence, waiting in anguish, as he continued.

"When you are ready, I will present myself for you to accept or reject. So for now I am content to remain your friend." Rising, he bade her goodnight and left.

Kandake's heart lurched at every beat. He had said what she wanted to hear. If she had left her breasts uncovered, tradition would have encouraged the response she wanted to give him. But she had not. She was not ready.

Until this moment she would have denied any interest in taking suitors; now she was not sure.

Amhara made all the difference. Thinking about him in this way caused Kandake to reconsider her decision.

When I decided to keep covered, I had not thought about this possibility, having feelings for someone. I have been training hard and focusing on improving my skills. It never occurred to me that you would be a possibility. And now, what I know is that when it is time I will tell you that I feel the same way. I will tell you that you will be the only one.

She shook her head. *Thinking about this or telling you that now will not help you or me. A warrior's strength is in earning what he desires. Waiting for it to be given is a sign of weakness. I know you, Amhara. You are warrior strong.*

Is this how Ezena feels about Nateka?

Rising from the water's edge, Kandake headed to her rooms for the evening. She had a lot to think about. Was she ready to accept the company of suitors? Would that change her desire to be a warrior? She entered the palace with her mind churning—thoughts of Amhara and concerns of the possibility of Nubia at war, or the kingdom being dragged into the battle of her neighbors. She made the last turn into the passageway that led to her rooms. Tabiry stood waiting, blocking Kandake's path.

"Tomorrow, Father decides Nubia's fate," Tabiry said. "You have to make sure he chooses what is best for all of us."

"What?" Kandake searched her sister's face to see if she was joking.

"He will listen to you. You are the one that will rule after him. It is as much your responsibility as his."

"I will rule after him, but it is not for me to advise him or direct the kingdom, now."

"It is not for you to receive suitors, either, but that did not stop you. I saw you sitting by the water with Amhara."

"Alara was with us. I have not done anything wrong."

"That is strange. I did not see our brother with you."

"Why would I lie, and to you?"

"I do not know. Maybe you have something to hide. Maybe you hid it from Great Mother and she missed it when she was planning who would be the one to rule after Father."

"Why do you always criticize everything I do?"

"Why do you always do things for me to criticize?" Tabiry folded her arms across her chest. She glared at Kandake and pointed to the knife she wore on her hip. "Look at you, even within the safety of the palace you walk about armed. Tell me, are you expecting another bandit attack? Here?"

"What?" Kandake threw up her arms in exasperation. "I do not need another argument. I am tired, Tabiry. If you have something to talk about other than how I am destroying the kingdom or killing innocent people, I will listen." She waited for her sister to speak. Tabiry stood there and glowered, saying nothing.

"Fine. I am going to bed." Kandake stepped around her to leave.

"I still do not understand why Great Mother chose you." Tabiry spat at her back.

"I do not know either." Kandake spun to face her sister. "Maybe it has something to do with my ability to handle my fears without searching for people to blame for what I cannot face." Kandake stepped closer. "Or maybe there is the possibility that I know how to wait and see what the outcome of a situation is before I decide the person in charge does not have the wisdom to choose well." She settled her hands on her hips. Her right hand rested on her knife. "Or just maybe it is because I am not afraid to do the hard thing."

_21_

The morning had been grueling and the afternoon promised to be no better. The air in the council chamber had already grown close, bordering on stifling. The aroma of the food at the side table had gone from appetizing to unappealing. Through all of it, Kandake continued to listen as members of the council expressed their opinion on what effect Nubian archers in Egypt would have on this kingdom.

"My King, we have to think of Nubia's economy," Uncle Naqa said, for the millionth time. "If we anger Egypt and they block the Nile on their end, Nubia will lose valuable trade."

"While there is merit to your argument," Uncle Dakká said, again countering his brother's position. "If Nubia aligns with Egypt in this, Assyria will read it as aggression against them and attack this kingdom. With our archers in Egypt we will not be strong enough to protect ourselves if we are attacked in force."

"So you say, but what will become of Nubia if there is no trade. In either case, we will be destroyed."

Oh, stop it, Kandake's brain screamed. *All this arguing back and forth is making my ears bleed. Please, somebody make a decision, will you!*

Her uncles had been going round and round with the same argument and that was getting them nowhere. She looked to see if her father was any closer in coming to a conclusion. His face gave away no clues. Looking to her aunt shed no information, either.

What was Father waiting for? What was the piece of information he needed to help him choose? Kandake searched her thoughts. Had there been anything that anyone had said to help them move forward?

"Both princes are right, My King." Aunt Alodia interrupted her brothers. "The answer does not lie in either argument. The solution is finding a way to combine them."

Kandake watched the light go on in her father's eyes. Then she saw him scrutinize his sister's face as if reading the solution in her features.

Because Alara studied with their aunt, Kandake looked at him hoping to find a trace of what her father was reading. But Alara's features appeared as blank as her mind felt. Natasen's expression was as fierce as Uncle Dakká's, but no hint of what the king thought. And Tabiry's face had the same strained appearance as Uncle Naqa's. It seemed that only Aunt Alodia and her father had any idea the direction the king was headed.

"Prince Dakká," King Amani turned to his brother. "How many units of archers can Nubia spare without weakening the kingdom?"

Kandake saw Uncle Dakká scowl. Then as if his face was made of melted wax, she watched the hard lines soften and flow into a knowing smile. Then her father turned to face his other brother.

"Prince Naqa," the king said. "What value would you lay on a Nubian archer? I want the amount paired with the changes of the moon."

A shrewd and knowing look came into the eyes of her uncle. His face no longer bore the expression of one whose loincloth had been twisted. The corners of his mouth lifted. His features took on that familiar look of setting a price the buyer would hate, but knew they would pay after all was said and done.

"We will end for the day," the king said. "Tomorrow we will review the information you both come up with."

The members of the council rose to leave. When Kandake stood, her father touched her arm indicating that she should stay behind with him. He waited until the room was clear of members and servants.

"Princess Kandake." Her father's voice took on the tone of instructor to student. "Two questions. Why has the king made this choice and how did he come to it?"

He thinks I know the answer to this? How could I?

She stroked the braid behind her ear while she considered his questions. The soft tinkle of bells at the end of the plait reminded her that the day would come when she would have to make a choice like this.

Okay, think. If he is asking me, then the answer is there for me to find, she encouraged herself. *Take your time and walk through it.*

Her father waited in his usual quiet patience, while Kandake puzzled through his questions. She recalled as much as she could about the arguments of her uncles. Thinking them through, she came to the same conclusion as her Aunt Alodia. They were both right.

So the answer lies in what would satisfy them both, which is protecting Nubia. For Uncle Dakká, protection means strength of force. For Uncle Naqa, it is strength of trade.

Once her thinking brought her this far, the answer stood out in plain sight. Kandake shifted her eyes to lock with her father's. He nodded his readiness to hear her answer. She explained.

"The answer is clear when you recognize that the arguments of both princes carry weight. They both want to protect Nubia, each in his own way. From there, it is only a matter of figuring out how to blend their suggestions.

"Prince Dakká knows exactly how many archers Nubia has and what the kingdom can afford to send to Egypt. By sending only this number, we are still at strength. Giving Egypt what it needs maintains the relationship between the two kingdoms, and as a bonus, it yields a profit for Nubia, which will certainly please Uncle Naqa."

"Well done, Princess Kandake," her father said, thumping the tabletop with the flat of his hand. "Great Mother is right. You will make a strong queen." He squeezed her shoulder as he rose. "Go, untangle your mind. Tomorrow's meeting promises to be just as demanding."

Kandake returned to her rooms. She sat on a bench beside a window and gazed out, taking in as much of the kingdom as her window would allow. Today's meeting had sucked huge amounts of energy from her. She felt wrung out like so much wet laundry.

I am as tired as if I had sparred all day, she thought. *Ruling, making the right choices for an entire kingdom requires a different kind of energy.*

A knot of small children caught her eye. She watched them playing a game that involved smooth stones, chasing one another, and a lot of squealing. They had no idea of the weighty things that were being decided in the council meetings. They played with the energy and freedom of those without cares. She felt the corners of her mouth pull into a smile remembering the days she used to play this same game.

Her eyes moved on, settling on a group of women sitting in the shade of a canopy of fabric with vibrant colors. They worked together stitching what looked to be another such awning. Two of the women had babies nursing at their breasts. Another had a young one sitting on the ground near her. He played with short strips of cloth tied together in large knots.

The women talked and laughed as they worked. Occasionally, the breeze would bring snatches of their conversation, sharing some of the bits of their lives with Kandake. A room added for a new baby. New lambs being born to the flock. A trade made for a breeding cow.

The life of Nubia stretched from her window. Council meetings and hard decisions ensured that her people and the rich culture continued. Her duty and love lived in the people beyond the palace.

My vow to you, Nubia, is everything that I am and all I do will keep you safe.

<u>22</u>

Things seem to be going well, so far, Kandake thought. She looked around the table and listened as her uncles made their presentations to her father. The room and the attendees were the same, but yesterday's tension seemed to have evaporated.

At least the arguing has stopped. Uncle Naqa seems pleased. He gets to keep the trade routes and add the profit from the archers to Nubia's treasure.

Kandake turned toward her other uncle. *He looks just as satisfied. Granting Egypt five units of archers and the compensation paid will not only feed their families while they are away, but will also add a goat to each archer's personal herd. And there is the payment of a cow for breeding for the family whose archer does not return.*

"It appears we have an answer for Egypt," King Amani said. "Princess Alodia, have the offer presented to Pharaoh with my seal.

"When Pharaoh agrees," the king continued, "Prince Dakká, I will need you to see to the rest." Her uncle nodded his agreement.

The discussion changed to the question of the bandits' identity. Kashta was invited to the council and brought a chest with him.

"After the prince left for the groves," Kashta said. "We examined the bodies of our attackers. And what we found was something of a puzzle." He bent to the chest and removed several of the items from inside.

"One would expect bandits to hide as much of their origin as possible, but what we found were these," Kashta said. He set the items on the table for all to see. One of them was a short sword, this he passed to King Amani. "It is a Sumerian dagger. Its identity is in the curvature of the blade. From this we were meant to think the bandits are Sumerian, or possibly Hittite, since they both carry weapons like these."

The king examined the weapon, noting the craftsmanship. He passed it on to Kandake's aunt. He signaled for Kashta to continue.

"This mace is definitely Egyptian, but the battle axe is Assyrian in construction." He handed these over for inspection, as well. "Now for their clothing. Their robes and sandals are from the lands beyond the Hittites."

"It would seem that someone went to a lot of trouble to confuse the situation," King Amani said. He passed the remainder of the items on for the others to examine. "It makes me wonder what exactly was the point of the attack?"

"That is what I have been trying to understand," Uncle Dakká said. "Looking at the whole of it, these were no ordinary bandits, if they were bandits at all. I have been reviewing the attack with my seniors. Robbery was not their purpose. Not only was nothing taken, they made no serious attempt to steal."

"Do you think they were trying to find the location of our groves?" Aunt Alodia asked.

"I do not think so," Kashta answered, folding his hands together. "There were no chipping tools among their belongings."

"So, what was the reason of the attack?" Uncle Naqa asked, his brows knit together and head cocked to the side. Every line of his body reflected the question of the others in the room.

"Exactly. What was the point?" Uncle Dakká said. "We think the situation goes beyond this one incident. We looked back over the past few months and figured in the increase in attacks along the trade route. There is much more than stealing going on."

The king's face took on a thoughtful expression. Kandake saw her aunt's features rearrange, mirroring her father's. In the silence, she could feel the tension rise in the room.

Something is going on and I am sure it is not at all good for this kingdom. Bandits that are not bandits. That cannot be good. And if they were not bandits, what were they? Where did they come from? And what did they want?

"You have their clothing, but what can you tell me about them?" The king leaned toward Kashta. "I need to know about these men. Something that will tell me where they are from. Something that will explain all of this." He gestured toward the objects they had collected

Kashta bowed his head in concentration. He stared at the tabletop as if reading the information. "There were twenty-three bandits in all. Their skin was the color of honeyed bread. Their eyes looked like circles pulled from the side, the shape of almonds. Dark hair with no curl."

"What of their speech?" the king asked. "What language did they use?"

"My King, I would have to say none engaged me other than my bow or knife."

"Did you hear their speech?" he asked, turning his eyes on Uncle Dakká. The prince shook his head.

"Excuse me, My King," Kandake interrupted. "The one who attacked me spoke." Her father's head whipped in her direction.

"Did you understand him? What did he say?"

"It was not difficult to understand what he said. He spoke our language, but with an accent. One I have not heard before."

"Princess, think carefully," Uncle Dakká said. "Tell us exactly what he said to you."

"When he saw that I was female, it surprised him. He called me some word that I could not recognize and spat on the ground."

She became lost in her thoughts. Talking about the incident brought back the emotion of the event, but without the previous intensity. Anger spread through her, recalling the insult.

"He said that he would snap me like a sapling." She hissed the remembered phrase through her teeth. Looking down at the tabletop, she saw her hands clenched into tight fists with knuckles threatening to puncture her skin.

"These men were not from the surrounding kingdoms," Aunt Alodia said. "It is well known that Nubian warriors are male and female."

"If they were not from the neighboring kingdoms, then where?" King Amani looked to the faces of those sitting at the table with him. "Who would profit most by attacking our caravans?"

"It was not just the caravan that they were attacking," Prince Dakká pointed out. "They were attacking Nubia. I do not believe they expected to find our warriors among the tradesmen. I think they were trying to weaken Nubia with fear."

"Weaken us, how?"

"By making us afraid to leave our borders. Making us fear that we cannot protect our own along the trade routes."

"If that is what they think…," the king began.

"My King?" Aunt Alodia interrupted him. "What if they are hoping to get Nubia to respond with force— trying to induce us to blame one of our neighbors for the attack? Was not the arrow pulled from Amhara, Egyptian?"

_23_

"If we had not been there to fight off the bandits…," Uncle Dakká said, following Aunt Alodia's line of thought.

"We would have assumed that the attackers were from Egypt," Uncle Naqa said. "But, who would want us to attack Egypt?"

"Maybe the better question is, who would gain the most if both kingdoms were tied up in a war against each other?" Her father's question had the face of everyone at the table frowning in thought or concentration.

Kandake's mind reached for answers. _If we had blamed Egypt for an attack on our caravan, what direction would all of this have taken? Would we go to war with a trusted neighbor? And if both kingdoms are focused on each other, as Father suggests, who stands to gain? What is the truth? Where were these attackers from?_

Kandake was yanked from her thoughts. She had not heard her father's question, but everyone was looking at her, waiting for her answer. Natasen, who was seated nearest her, whispered,

"The king asked where you thought the bandits came from."

"Given the color of their skin," she said, stalling and scampering through her thoughts to find the answer, "I would have to say that they come from the north. Likely, farther than Assyria." The heads around the table nodded their agreement.

"Anything else?" King Amani asked.

"The shape of their eyes is as unfamiliar as their speech. So, I do not believe we have had many dealings with wherever they were from."

"Prince Natasen." The king turned to face his youngest son. "What can you add?"

"I would have to agree with Princess Kandake. We do not recognize them by features or by speech. And their surprise that Kandake is female says that they are not familiar with us or our ways."

"If we do not know them and they are not familiar with us...." The king turned his attention toward his other daughter, "Can you tell me, Princess Tabiry, what do you think they want from Nubia?"

Tabiry sat without saying a word for a moment, as if gathering her thoughts. Then, she sat up, her back rod straight and gave the king her answer.

"The riches that gather in Nubia are well known. We trade well with our neighbors and with the kingdoms beyond. If someone could grasp

Nubia, they would have the wealth to conquer many kingdoms."

At the last, the king's attention rested upon Alara. "And now, Prince Alara, what can you tell me about this situation?"

The prince held his father's eyes as he spoke. "It would seem, My King, that there is a larger plan. And Nubia seems to be a small, but vital, part." Alara took a large swallow from his drink. "An impressive kingdom has threatened to attack our strongest neighbor without threat or warning to us. Our caravans are attacked with increasing fervor, not to take our goods, but to test our strength. And the attackers are men we do not know. From a land we do not know."

Alara gazed at the papyrus sheet upon which he had scribbled a few notes. "But they knew enough about our strength to bring twenty-three against a handful of tradesmen. And spoke enough of our language to insult and threaten Princess Kandake. Someone is teaching them about Nubia. Someone who wants to remain invisible to us, for now."

When Alara had finished, Kandake realized that there was no mistaking it. The threat of war hung over her home. She wondered if the others had come to this same conclusion. She watched a knowing glance exchange between Uncle Dakká and Kashta. It was all she needed to feel certain her conclusion was correct.

Alara and Aunt Alodia murmured as they scanned her pages of notes. Tabiry and Uncle Naqa appeared to review his calculations of the profit to be gained from the archers.

Even the faces of the servants appeared to express the weight of what was to come to Nubia.

"All of this said," King Amani recalled the attention of everyone. "What is the best strategy for Nubia?" The king looked to each face around the table. "I think it wise to keep our neighbor strong. So the archers go to Egypt without delay. This will also add strength to the alliance between the two kingdoms." He nodded to his sister indicating that his wishes should be carried out without delay.

"Now we move forward to protect the kingdom. If war is coming to Nubia, who will be the one to bring it? That seems to be our biggest question. Its answer will tell us how to prepare. What I need from all of you are thoughts on how to make the invisible seen? But now, I need to speak with my children. The council will convene in three days."

As the council rose to leave, King Amani dismissed the servants. He motioned for his children to sit close to him.

"It looks like what no one wants for Nubia may come," he told them, making eye contact with each of his children. "What this kingdom needs, more than ever, is for each of us to strengthen all of our relationships. As my children, everyone will be taking their lead from you about the condition of, and the hope for, Nubia."

Kandake felt herself fill with resolve and purpose. Her heart beat stronger with love for her home and its people.

"Princess Kandake," King Amani said, turning his full attention upon her. "Your job will be the most difficult. As next to rule, your character and your strength will be scrutinized during these strenuous times. Your judgment must be impeccable. If your faith in the outcome of Nubia wavers, then the people's faith in you will waver. Should this happen, their hope in Nubia will die. And if that occurs, we are all lost."

Her father's fierce expression drove the seriousness of the situation, and her role in it, into Kandake's heart. The force of it pierced through her core. Then he turned to the remainder of his children.

"All of Nubia will be watching how you support their next queen. If you hesitate, or falter, in this in any way, the throne of Nubia will crumble. Your backing of the kingdom's next queen must be solid.

"May I have your word that you will support and serve your queen?" King Amani's eyes elicited confirmation from each of his children in their turn.

Kandake studied each of their faces. Alara's features held his usual solemn support as he gave his assent. Natasen's face displayed fierce solidarity when giving his word. And when Tabiry agreed her expression was, once more, carefully neutral.

<u>24</u>

It had been less than two months since the attack, but things seemed like business as usual for Kandake as she attended weekly council meetings. Once Pharaoh agreed to the conditions, Uncle Dakká and Kashta selected the archers that would travel to Egypt. Uncle Naqa was impressed that Egypt had not quibbled over his set fee. Not only that, Pharaoh sent King Amani gold, jewels, linen, and several healthy cows as a gift of the alliance between the two kingdoms.

Everything appeared to be going well except that there were no new clues as to the origin of the attackers. For now, the focus was on properly outfitting the archers before they left.

"Prince Dakká, be sure that each archer has a second bow and three bow strings," the king reminded his brother. "And in their provisions, add three bushels of new shafts. Nubian arrows must fly straight."

"It has been taken care of, My King." Taking his list from Kashta, Uncle Dakká read aloud the supplies he was planning to send with the archers. "They will have to eat the Egyptian food, but each archer will carry his own pouch of medicines."

"It seems we have done all we can for them," King Amani said. "How soon will they leave?"

"Pharaoh is sending a barge," Princess Alodia said. "Our archers are to board it at the end of this week."

"If I may make a suggestion?" Uncle Dakká asked his brother. "I am not sure it is wise to have so many Nubian archers in one place. All anyone would have to do is sink the barge and we would lose all of them."

"What would you suggest?"

"Send half the archers on the barge, but the remainder travel by horseback over our lands to Egypt."

While the king contemplated his brother's suggestion, Kandake's mind wrangled with the implications.

Uncle Dakká is still worried that the arrow in Amhara's side was Egyptian in make and responsibility. If he really thinks they are behind the attacks on the caravans, why send the archers at all?

"Good plan," King Amani said. "Have one of the archers carry a message telling Pharaoh where to meet the rest of them. Nubia needs to exercise wisdom and caution in her dealings."

After the meeting ended, Kandake went in search of relaxation. Taking her fishing nets and a small meal wrapped in a bundle, she headed for her favorite spot along the Nile. Before she could make her escape from the palace, Tabiry stood at the doorway.

"Going out for pleasure instead of trying to learn the identity of our enemies," Tabiry accused, pointing at Kandake's fishing nets. "It is just like you. Have you got what you wanted? Are you happy, now?"

"And what is it you think I want?"

"Everyone's looking under bushes and rocks to find an enemy that probably does not exist. Uncle Dakká is even ready to blame our neighbor for the attack on your friend."

"How is any of this what I want?" Kandake felt her temper rising.

"A war is the perfect opportunity to prove yourself as a warrior. Well then, Warrior Queen, prove yourself. Go find our real enemies instead of wasting your time playing with fishing nets. You ought to be doing something useful. You could be out with Alara in the hunt adding to the kingdom's supply of fresh meat or at least protecting them while they are out there." She waved her hand in the air. "What if his party runs into the bandits or worse?"

Kandake's irritation peaked. She took a step closer to her sister to tell her what she really thought. She drew breath to let her words fly, but remembered her father's instruction—*your character must be impeccable*.

Breathe, Kandake breathe. She worked to regain control of her temper. *Tabiry is no different than she has always been. You cannot let her make you angry.*

Kandake released her breath in silence. She stepped around Tabiry and used warrior discipline to change her mood. She walked out of the palace and into the city beyond. As she traveled, she made a point of speaking to everyone she passed.

A group of young children were playing a game of stone pitches. She remembered enjoying this game when she was younger. Kandake asked if she could play.

"You will have to be on their team," one of the children said, pointing to the other group. "We are winning and someone as old as you might make us lose."

"I see," Kandake said, maintaining a serious expression. She turned to the leader of the other team. "May I play on your team?"

"I guess so," he told her, reluctance written in every line of his posture. "But you will throw last. That way if it takes you too many tries to hit the gourd, no one will lose their turn."

"I promise to do my best."

She waited in silent patience until every one had pitched. Her side was behind by two points. It was clear that they thought they had already lost and passed her the pitching stones. If she hit the gourd, it would be worth two points and the game would be tied.

Positioning the stone in her hand so that the flat side was parallel with the ground, Kandake hurled it. It skimmed just above the dust, hitting the gourd, causing it to skip and topple over.

"Three points!" her team leader yelled. "We win!"

Kandake cheered with her teammates, but celebrated with all of the children. She unwrapped her bundle and gave each child a honeyed date, which they ate together sitting in the dust. As she left the group she heard one of them whisper, "I told you we should have taken her for our team. She is a warrior. Nubian warriors do not miss."

The worst of the day's heat was over. Moisture from the Nile had a cooling effect near the water's edge. Studying the shoreline for the best place to drop her nets, Ezena and Natasen joined her. Natasen took one of her nets and cast it out for her while she flung the other. Waiting for her catch, they sat on the ground and shared what was left in her small bundle of food.

The dust of the ground where they sat was fine but packed hard from the feet of the many fishermen who trod over this spot. Natasen leaned back on his elbows watching hawks wheeling over the opposite shoreline. Soon, one of the birds flung back its wings and lowered its head in a speed dive. Just before reaching the water's surface, it pulled its wings forward and thrust its talons into the river, snatching up its prey. "That is the way we will find our attackers," Natasen said, admiring the bird's technique. "We will wait for them to make their next move. And just like that hawk, we will strike before they know we have seen them."

"But the hawk knows where to watch," Kandake said, getting up to check her nets. "We still do not know where these men come from."

"They are different enough that they cannot hide for long," Ezena said. "Someone will talk about seeing the strangers and it will get back to us." She helped Kandake sort the fish in her net, throwing back the ones that were too small.

Kandake transferred all but three of the fish to one net. After weighting it and tying it off, she returned the full net to the water to preserve her catch. Ezena and Natasen cleaned the fish while Kandake built a fire to cook them.

"Wish I could have gone with Alara," Natasen said, scraping the scales from the fish. "He's out there hunting and I am stuck here training. Uncle Dakká has me working twice as hard as before. Whoever these strangers are, when I catch up with them, they will pay for every drop of sweat, every missed hunt, and every long day of studying strategies because of them." He threw a stone into the water, hard.

"What are you complaining about?" Kandake turned the fish sizzling on the hot rocks. "I have Tabiry in my ear going on about my 'not doing anything useful.'"

"What does she want you to do?" Ezena asked.

"She said I should have at least gone with Alara on the hunt. According to her, if I went with him I could search for the bandits while I am out there, since I have nothing to do. She implied that I should have gone to protect Alara and those with him.

"How can she say I have nothing to do? I have father and Uncle Dakká drilling me. My body and my mind have been worked to exhaustion every day. And now Aunt Alodia, too. She is supposed to be teaching me about diplomacy and strange cultures. What does a warrior need to know about diplomacy?"

"You are right, a warrior has little need of diplomacy." Kandake's friend elbowed her playfully in the side. "But a queen does."

25

Returning to her studies in the palace, Kandake handed the net of fresh fish to a servant to take to the kitchen. She sought out her aunt's rooms, resigning herself to the hours of study ahead.

Diplomacy. Kandake had no use for the concept. *A warrior is strong. Her words are direct. How is learning to talk around a subject helpful? Talk does not turn away an attacking army from our borders. Those bandits did not have much to say, and they were not listening, either.*

She entered her aunt's work area, bowed in respect, and then joined her at the large table littered with scrolls and tablets. The walls around them were covered with maps, new and old, of the surrounding kingdoms. The room had a light, musky smell of old cured hides. The coverings at the windows were tied back, letting in maximum light.

"Princess Kandake," her aunt said. "I want you to study these." Aunt Alodia indicated a pile of scrolls that had been stacked in a criss-cross fashion keeping them in place. Kandake groaned and took the seat in front of the heap.

"Aunt Alodia, what are in these?" she asked, breaking the seal of the first one.

"They are the histories of ancient wars, what caused them and how they were ended. The one in your hand tells of the wars before Nubia was united."

Kandake spread the scroll out in front of her. She paid close attention to the words and subtle nuances of the original insults perceived on both sides. It amazed her that the simple misunderstanding of a gift could bring about such hostility that ended up causing a war.

"How could this happen?" she asked. "This was not worth fighting over. People died. Why? Because a goat was given when a cow was promised?"

"Something like that. In short, the lesser chieftain had promised the greater chieftain a cow, a load of copper, and the technique for hardening arrow shafts. He brought the greater chieftain all that he had promised with the exception of the cow. The cow had died and the lesser chieftain replaced it with a goat."

"I understand that a goat does not have the same value as a cow, but is it cause for war?"

"The greater chieftain assumed the lesser was calling him stupid. It had something to do with an old rivalry. Nevertheless, that was not the lesser chieftain's intention, as was determined after the end of their war. Then it was explained that because of the death of the cow, the goat was given as a pledge against a promise that as soon as another cow calved it would be given to that chieftain."

"So, what happened?"

"The answer is here." Her aunt handed Kandake another scroll that contained the history of how the peace was restored and the joining of the two villages.

By the end of their study period Kandake had read until her eyes were burning and dry. She took the scrolls Aunt Alodia sent with her to study. Dropping the bundle off in her rooms, Kandake went to the kitchens and asked for a platter of food for her evening meal. She took it to the courtyard to eat in the open air and watch the sun set.

Finding a spot on the portico with the best view, Kandake sat with her back supported by a column. She gazed out over the distance, watching the sun make its descent as it smudged the sky with streaks of orange, pink, and purple. Allowing her tension to decline with the sun, Kandake began her meal. The bite of roasted meat with herbs danced across her tongue as the sharp cheese blended with the meat's flavor. Sinking her teeth into the flesh of a fresh fig was a flavorful accompaniment to the previous savory mouthful.

"So this is where you are hiding," Tabiry said. "I have been looking for you everywhere."

It was good while it lasted. Kandake moaned, set her plate aside, but remained seated. "What do you want, Tabiry?" Her sister's face was twisted in irritation. Kandake wondered what she could have done to cause her sister to break with her evening ritual of grinding colored gems into the fine dust she would use to paint her eyelids in the morning.

"Father sent me to find you," her sister huffed. "You may have been selected as the next queen, but today, I am still your older sister."

"My older sister?" Kandake asked, not understanding where the conversation was going or what it was about.

"Yes, your older sister. Why should I trek all over the kingdom looking for you? I am not yours to command. Or are you dispensing with tradition already, having the older serve the younger."

Kandake chose not to remind Tabiry that their father had sent her. It was his authority she was obeying. Getting to her feet she asked, "Do you know what he wants?"

"That is not my position, either. Go find out for yourself."

Kandake went in search of her father. She found him in the chamber off the throne-room sitting in his seat at the head of the table. Her Uncle Dakká and Kashta were seated with him. Their heads were bowed in low conversation. Concern was written in her father's features. He looked up as she walked through the doorway.

"Princess Kandake." Her father gestured to the seat nearest him. "Please sit with us."

She took the seat at her father's right hand. A servant brought her a small plate of fruit slices and a cool drink of water. Kandake took a swallow of the water. "You sent for me?"

"Did Alara say if he was spending the night away with the hunt?"

"No. He has not returned?"

"He has not," her uncle said. "Nor has he told anyone that he would be away for the night. It is not like him."

"No, it is not," she muttered to herself. "Do you think he was hurt? I am sure he will send someone to let us know."

"Natasen was with you earlier," her father said. "Did he say anything about Alara not returning until morning?"

"No, he did not." She pushed away from the table. "I will be ready to track his party as soon as I get my bow and sling."

"I have a team ready to leave," Uncle Dakká said. "We were just waiting to hear if you had any information."

"It will only take me a moment." She headed for the door.

"Princess Kandake!" Her father barked her name in command, stopping her in her stride. "If there is something wrong, it will not be safe for you to leave the kingdom." She turned to argue with him. He held up his hand to cut her off. "Your place is here. I will not risk Nubia's next queen."

Kandake's eyes locked with her father's. Her brother needed her to help the others track him. If the strangers were involved, Alara could be in danger. *Maybe Tabiry was right, I should have gone with him.* She needed to get out there to find him, to make sure he was all right. *He has to be all right.* A queen waits but a warrior moves. Today, she was a warrior.

26

Kandake resumed her seat next to her father. Her resolve was clear. She was not about to be put off providing the help her brother must be in need of. She leveled her eyes with his. "Father, I have honored you in all that you have asked. Please do not ask this of me."

"I am not asking you," her father said, returning her gaze. "Your kingdom requires your protection in this."

"Every person of Nubia is due our protection," Kandake answered him. Her hands closed into tight fists on the table in front of her. "You are asking me to think of Nubia's coming future by turning my back on one of its citizens today."

"We are not turning our backs on Alara!"

She saw pain highlight her father's eyes.

The air hummed with the tension between Kandake and the king like hundreds of bee's wings confined in a small box.

"Princess Kandake," her uncle intervened. His tone was the same as he used in training sessions. "A warrior waits for all available information before making a decision. A band of men is being dispatched to search for the prince. The king is asking that you remain in the palace until they return."

Kandake listened to her uncle's voice. The authority intertwined within the words reminded her of her duties as a warrior. With a command, she quieted the edge of rage rising inside her. She forced her hands to release their grip, as if they held onto her resolve to find her brother. She laid them on her lap.

"My King," Kandake said, turning repentant eyes upon her father. "I ask your pardon. I have not behaved as a warrior should."

"There is no need for pardon." Her father took one of her hands in both of his. "You acted like a sister who loves her brother. But during times like these, Nubia needs you to act like a warrior who will protect her kingdom and a queen who will make the best decision for everyone."

At her father's permission, Kandake took her leave of them and headed toward her mother's rooms. Along the way, she asked a servant to bring a tray with a pitcher of cool water and plates of honeyed figs and salted nuts, her mother's favorites.

She found Tabiry sitting at their mother's feet, crying a river whose flow was rivaled only by that of the Nile.

"What if he is hurt or dead?" her sister wailed.

"I am sure he is fine," their mother soothed. "The greater likelihood is that he found a trail that took him farther than he had planned and is waiting until daylight to return."

"But what if you are wrong?"

"Mother is right," Kandake interjected, coming to sit on the bench in front of her sister. "Alara is fine. I am sure it is as she says."

Kandake stretched her arm across her mother's shoulders. She could feel knots of tension beneath the skin of her neck and back. Even though she had not spoken of her great concern for her son, the bunched muscles communicated the extent of her worry to her daughter.

The servant entered the room with the tray Kandake had requested and set it on a low table nearby. Dismissing her, Kandake poured her mother and sister shallow bowls of the cool water. Handing one to each, she encouraged them to drink. Seeing that they followed her instructions, she refilled their bowls.

"This is what is happening," she began. She told her mother and sister what her father and Uncle Dakká had decided. "So we should know something by morning."

"It will be a very long night," her mother said.

# # # #

Not long after sunrise, Kandake entered the king's chamber to wait for news about Alara. Natasen was already seated at the table.

"Did you sleep at all?" Natasen asked, studying Kandake's face. He poured his sister a mixture of pomegranate juice and water and slid it to her.

"A little. I have been thinking most of the night. Wondering what could have happened to him."

"His practice is that if he is going to be out longer than he anticipated, he sends one of the servants back with the message." Natasen locked his eyes with his sister's. "I do not like it. I do not like it at all."

She nodded her head in agreement. "Something is not right."

King Amani entered the room. Kandake and her brother stood in respect; he waved them back to their seats. He looked haggard, a sign that he had not slept. A servant placed a small plate of food before him. He waved it away, but accepted a vessel of the cool, thinned juice.

"My King," Uncle Dakká addressed his brother as he entered the room. "A rider has returned with some news." The king urged him to continue.

"The warriors have found the cart tracks where the carcasses of the hunt were loaded." This information might have been helpful had Kandake not read the concern in her uncle's features. The unspoken 'but' hung in the air.

"And signs of my son?" King Amani asked, worry etching his face.

"Nothing, yet," he told his brother. "It appears they loaded their kill and moved on. The rest of the warriors are still following the tracks."

There is something you are not saying, Uncle. Kandake waited. She knew there was more to come. She listened while he finished his report, holding fear at bay. She wanted to know what he was not saying, but if she started asking questions, would he tell her things she did not want to hear? Kandake turned toward her father. She could see the king and her brother hanging onto every word her uncle said. She knew her uncle well and read the concern in his face.

"There is no sign of struggle found. It may be that Alara just decided to extend his hunt."

It was the best Uncle Dakká could offer the king. He seemed to accept his brother's words.

Kandake saw that a bit of the fear had left her father's eyes.

We all know Alara better than that. He would have sent a message, but if this eases Father, I will accept it. She needed to loosen the grip fear had on her heart but could not. Something was wrong.

Kandake chose to accept the comfort her uncle was offering, but it was hollow. She caught Natasen's eyes. As the council meeting began, she signaled to him that they would meet later to talk afterwards.

# # # #

"What did you think of the meeting?" Kandake asked Natasen. They met in the fields near the stables where there was little chance that they would be overheard.

"I noticed that no one mentioned Alara," Natasen said. "We are all worried, but no one is talking about it. Everyone is on edge."

"Aunt Alodia is so tense her back is as stiff as ebony."

"Uncle Naqa looks like someone has sucked all of the air out of him. He sags all over. It is like he does not have any bones. And it is clear to see Tabiry cried all night."

"Not much news there. She cries over the least thing," Natasen said.

"I know, but she did not bother to paint her eyelids this morning," Kandake added. "This is not her usual moodiness, she is really worried."

"So what are we going to do about it?" Natasen said. "I cannot sit and do nothing."

"Neither can I, but without more to go on, we do not even know where to start looking." Kandake squeezed the handful of sand she held, and then pitched it away from her. "We will have to wait for Senka and the others to come back. Then we will know what we need to do and where to do it."

"I will accept that—for now." He shook his head. "But the moment I know where to look…." Agitated, Natasen pulled his knife from the casing at his hip and tested its edge against the hair on his arm. The blade left a clean swath of skin. He returned it to its sheath, but his hand hovered nearby.

Kandake watched her brother's movements. Motions that had once been buoyant and fluid were now keen and precise. Each gesture had the look of an arrow seeking its objective.

Her heart read their meaning; someone would pay if their brother had been harmed.

Kandake hated the fear she had read in her parents' eyes since Alara went missing. It burned like fire in her veins. She only knew one way to quench that flame. She would see her brother home. He would be safe and unharmed or her own arrow would find its mark.

27

That evening, Abu, one of the warriors searching with Senka, brought the news that they had found one of Alara's servants. But he was injured and could not be moved. Abu had been sent to fetch a healer to see to his needs.

Uncle Dakká questioned Abu until late into the night, but he was not able to give much information. Senka had dispatched him for the healer the moment they discovered the servant still lived.

Kandake listened as her uncle reported all that Abu had told him. Everyone listened with such intensity, that the air around them seemed held by their focus. At the end of his narration, Uncle Dakká leaned against the back of his seat like a sail that had lost its wind.

"How long before they return with the servant?" King Amani asked.

"That will depend upon what the healer sees. All we can do now is wait for their return."

The king nodded his acceptance that all that was possible was being done. "And what of our archers? Is there any news from the north?"

"Nedjeh has returned with the horses. He reports that the archers on the barge arrived safely and met them at the border."

"That is good news." The king sat in quiet thought, staring at the tabletop.

Kandake wondered what images passed through her father's mind. Did he see Alara wounded like she imagined the servant? Did he see his body lying lifeless on a bloodstained patch of ground?

No! I will not think that. She brought her mind's musing under discipline. *I will not ever believe that unless I see it with my own eyes. A warrior does not fear what she has not seen. I am a warrior.*

# # # #

Two days after the healer left to join the search party, Uncle Dakká received word that the servant was well enough to travel. Kandake was sitting with her mother when the news reached her.

"Did they say how long it would be before they arrived?" her mother asked. Kandake could see that tension and strain were carving their presence into Queen Sake's face.

"It will be at least another day, Mother," Kandake said. "They will have to move at a gentler pace than we would like. I am told that the servant's injuries were severe. He had been left for dead."

"Oh," was her mother's only response before she returned to her work. Kandake had never thought of her parents aging before, but Alara's disappearance had brought shadows to their eyes.

She watched her mother perform her usual duties, rotating fresh supplies of medicines and foods for those in storage. Written on the stacks of papyrus sheets, hides, and earthen tablets covering the tabletops were lists of what was held in stores for Nubia. Queen Sake usually kept these around her for ease of reference, but almost never needed them. Kandake noted that today her mother depended upon the reference lists. Without question, Alara's absence was taking its toll.

Studies with her father continued in the usual routine, but it was clear to Kandake that worries about her brother distracted him, too. Addressing issues of Nubia's citizenry from his throne lacked his typical keenness.

Everyone was performing their duties and going about their business like normal, yet there was nothing normal about the day. The air was filled with uncertainty. Unspoken questions were stuffed into every corner and crevice of space. Who had attacked her brother? Why? Was Alara safe? Had they harmed him? Who would dare?

I, Princess Kandake, the next queen of Nubia, vow that if Alara has been harmed, I will teach those responsible why the bow of Nubia is rightly feared. Her promise of punishment for anyone who would harm her brother settled her spirit.

Kandake yanked her concentration back to her father, learning from the decisions he made for the kingdom. But everything around her reminded her of Alara. He was the soothing balm for her just as Aunt Alodia was to her father. Only today, Kandake was not sure of her aunt's effectiveness. She could see her aunt wrestling with her own agitation.

The clatter of sandals rushing over the stone floor grabbed her attention. A warrior covered in dust and appearing weary from a long ride was ushered in to the king. As the warrior dropped to one knee and bowed in respect, she lost her balance. King Amani commanded, another to help her to her feet.

"My King," she said, her voice only just above a whisper. It carried the tone of dried reeds scrubbing against more dried reeds. "I have come from our neighbor to the north. The Assyrians have attacked the southern portion of Egypt's eastern border."

"Call Prince Dakká at once," King Amani bellowed, his voice filling the room. "Thank you for your diligence. See to it that this warrior is fed and rested."

Uncle Dakká came into the throne-room at a run. "My King, you called?" Kandake's uncle dropped to one knee as he spoke.

"It appears Egypt's enemies may attempt to penetrate Nubia from the north. Strengthen that border." As her father gave the order, she saw some of life's light return to his eyes.

"It is done," Uncle Dakká said, departing with fierce purpose and will scribed in the line of his back.

War had arrived in Nubia. The atmosphere bristled with excitement. It gave people something to worry about other than Alara. This was an enemy they could confront, an attack they understood. Kandake watched as her father issued orders. Those in his presence followed them. The anxious lethargy that had settled over everyone like an unctuous mantle evaporated.

"The council will convene within one quarter of an hour," her father announced as he left the throne room. Kandake took that as a signal to escape to her grandmother's rooms for a quick conversation.

She found her grandmother sitting on large pillows gazing out over Nubia through her window. Kandake knelt at her side, waiting to be acknowledged.

"Have you forgiven me, yet?" Kandake's grandmother asked the question without turning from her view.

"Great Mother, there is nothing to forgive." Kandake handed her the package of dried figs she had brought. "I was never angry with you. It is just that I wanted something else for my life. I still do not understand why you chose me."

Her grandmother took the gift, opened the package, and shared the fruit with her granddaughter. Kandake chewed the sticky flesh and crunched its seeds. Waiting for her grandmother's response, she, too, gazed out of the window. Her vision took in all of the things she treasured about her home: the people, the way Nubia's children were cared for by everyone, and the strength of Nubia's culture. She knew of no other kingdom where a mother could leave her child with a stranger and when she returned she would find that child safe and well cared for. Where else could she find a people so strong? In what other kingdom could a woman choose her life to be or do what pleased her, even being a warrior?

"I chose you because of your love for all of this," her grandmother said as she released what sounded like a long held breath. "I chose you because of what is happening now."

"But they love Nubia, too, Great Mother." Kandake searched her grandmother's face. "Alara, and Natasen, would easily die for Nubia. Even Tabiry would rather die than see Nubia come to an end."

"Alara works best with his mind. He understands people, but sometimes he is slow to respond when others wrong him. Natasen is different than Alara. He understands people well, but he responds a little too quickly to an affront."

Her grandmother left the window and seated herself on a pillow in a cooler part of the room. "And then there is Tabiry. She believes others think the way she does or that they should. It never occurs to her that someone else's motives may be different than her own. What is worse, she allows fear to determine her course."

Kandake left the window. She opened her mouth to object, but closed it. The description of her sister was accurate, but it pricked to hear those words from someone she respected. "What about me causes you to believe I would rule any better than my brothers?"

"Because you are who you have always been. Just now, even though I told the truth about Tabiry, it riled you, yet you held your tongue. This is the reason.

"You listen for the truth and accept it. When there is something to be done, no matter how difficult, you see it through to the end. War has come to Nubia. This kingdom will require great things from its rulers, if it is to survive."

"But, Great Mother, great things come from great rulers. I am not sure I can become that." Kandake let her gaze fall to the floor. Embarrassment, for what she believed was her lacking swallowed her. Doubt became her second skin. Before her lay an expectation that she worried she could not meet.

"Princess Kandake!" Her grandmother's sharp voice commanded her attention. Kandake snapped her chin back up and brought her eyes level with the strong woman facing her. "This is not something that you must become. It is what you are."

28

Kandake sat listening to Uncle Dakká give the details about the incursion on Nubia's northeastern border. He updated her father on the number and placement of warriors and their reinforcements.

"I believe that will hold the perimeter for now," Uncle Dakká said. "It will take a day or more to determine their level of commitment to invading the kingdom."

A messenger slipped into the room and handed a note to a servant, who passed it to Kashta. After reading it, he mumbled something to her uncle. At his sharp intake of breath, all eyes in the room landed upon him.

"My King, I have received word that Prince Alara's servant has arrived and has been taken to the healer's home."

"Has he said anything about my son?" The king's face held hope and fear. Anguish hovered at the corners of his eyes.

"He has not said anything, yet. The healer has not been able to awaken him."

"I want a runner placed at his side to notify me the moment he rouses."

Uncle Dakká dispatched a servant to carry out the king's orders.

"My King," Kandake interjected into the quiet of the servant's departure. "I would be willing to sit at his side." She needed to be near anyone or anything that brought her closer to her brother. She and Natasen shared the same spirit, but Alara's presence always comforted her.

"Thank you, Princess Kandake, but your presence is needed here."

Kandake worked to keep the disappointment from her face. She knew her father was right, but waiting for the news was agony.

"It would seem that the moment I feared for Nubia has arrived." The king panned the table and locked gazes with each one in turn. "Nubia has a threat knocking at its door. The double threat is that my son has not been accounted for, and from the condition of his servant, Alara appears to be in some danger."

Kandake felt the muscles in her back tighten. Her right hand came to rest upon the knife she wore at her side. She glanced across the table at Natasen; the fierce gleam she saw in his eyes matched what she felt in her heart.

The only hair missing from his head had better be no more than that which he has chosen to shave. And any blood let from his body, no more than a nick from his shaving. Kandake found her teeth gnashing to the cadence of her thoughts. She tapped a modified tempo of this rhythm on the casing of her knife. Her father's voice sharpened her attention to what was being said.

"First priority is to ensure that Nubia's borders are strong. I want patrols at regular intervals. All visitors to the kingdom are to be identified and escorted by our warriors." The king continued issuing orders that would guarantee the safety of all within the kingdom. In his final order, he said, "The poorer families of Nubia are to be fed from my herds. I do not want anyone hunting alone during this danger."

Everyone present wrote down what they needed to carry out their portion of the king's orders. When the meeting ended, Kandake went in search of work to keep her mind from fretting over her missing brother. Her feet took her to the warriors' compound.

Laid out in a u-shape, the area was comprised of two long, low buildings used as housing for warriors on either side of a wide courtyard. At the bottom of the u-shape stood a structure larger and taller than the rest. She stepped inside. Kandake had spent many hours in this building training, sparring, learning to use the weapons and the equipment to make them.

She crossed the expanse of the sparring floor, walked through the armory, and headed to the back area. The empty space was hot and the air damp. She could smell the sweat of warriors, evidence of recent practice. She itched to spar with someone herself. Each person she encountered sketched a bow and hustled past her, doing whatever their duty required in preparing for the protection and defense of the kingdom.

She exited the rear of the building. Artisans worked the rigs set up for smelting the iron that went into their weapons. They stopped to acknowledge her as she passed. Outside, Kandake found Amhara, busy at the painstaking task of straightening shafts for arrows. He turned lengths of green wood over a candle flame, rubbing and pulling, encouraging the piece to proper alignment. Afterwards, he hardened them in a slow process to make them strong enough to perform their duty. The number of shafts in his basket indicated he had been at his task for some time. She picked up a sack of feathers, a shallow basket, and sat on the ground next to him.

"I hear Alara has not come back yet," Amhara said, keeping his eyes on the shaft he was turning. "And that his servant is in the healer's house."

"Father is waiting for him to wake up. We cannot know anything of what happened to my brother until his servant is able to speak."

"When the king finds out, what will he do?"

"That is hard to say with the skirmish in the north. The security of Nubia comes first." The truth of those last words burned Kandake's throat as they came out. She hated to admit it, but Nubia's safety did come before her brother's. The weight of the circle of gold at her ankle seemed to have grown throughout this incident.

She grasped a goose feather by its quill. With a deft movement, she pinched and stripped the vane from it and placed the two halves in the basket in her lap. Kandake and Amhara worked in the quiet bustle of the compound. Around them warriors rushed about their tasks without unnecessary conversation. Neither took their eyes from their work, but Kandake felt soothed by Amhara's presence. She moved only to retrieve another bag of feathers when the first one was finished.

When Kandake was halfway through the second sack, one of the king's messengers burst from the rear of the building coming straight toward her. The messenger knelt before Kandake as he would the king.

Given permission, he rose to deliver his message. "Your father, the king, has sent me to find you, Princess," the servant spoke in a breathless rush. "The servant to Prince Alara has awakened and you are needed."

With the fluidity of well-trained muscles, Kandake sprinted for her father. She did not take the time to acknowledge receiving the servant's message. Nor did she say anything to her friend.

Running at full tilt, she collided with Natasen entering their mother's rooms. The sight in front of Kandake filled her mind with one thought. The thing she had prayed would never happen. What lay before her, the king on his knees before their mother, holding her as she wept filled Kandake's heart with dread.

29

Kandake and Natasen took slow, measured steps to join their father. They knelt with him at Queen Sake's feet. Soon afterwards, Tabiry joined them and began to wail. Her keening demanded their father's attention.

"Princess Tabiry," King Amani said. "Take hold of yourself. Stop your bawling. You sound like a cow stuck in the mud."

"How can I help it when my brother…," she choked out between sobs.

"Your brother, what?" her father said. His annoyance with Tabiry's behavior was evident.

"He is not…. But I saw Mother crying. I thought…," Tabiry stammered.

"Your mother is crying because we have news that Alara may be unharmed."

Kandake wondered if her eyes were bulging like her sister's at the king's news. She had feared, like Tabiry, that all was lost. But with her father's words, hope entered the room like a welcome breeze, one cooled by the Nile.

"I called you here so that I could tell you in private."

"Please, Amani," their mother pleaded. "Go on, tell me everything."

The king sat on the bench next to his wife. Natasen, Tabiry, and Kandake sat at his feet, listening to every word.

"Alara's party split into three groups. Each hunted along a different trail. They had planned to bring down several animals at once. Alara believed this would be his last opportunity to hunt beyond our borders because of the trouble coming to Egypt. He wanted to bring as much fresh meat to the kingdom as possible."

King Amani passed a hand over his weary face. He turned to hold his wife's gaze with his own. "His prediction was right. I had planned to prohibit anyone from hunting in unprotected areas."

Their father stretched his long legs between Tabiry and Kandake. He continued. "The servant reported that they were set upon without warning. Their attackers stripped them of all weapons and bound them at the wrists and ankles. Then they were marched off, tethered one to the other. It appears their attackers had knowledge that Alara is my son and believe him to be next in line for Nubia's throne."

"But how did the servant get away?" Natasen asked.

"When they stopped to water the animals, they untied the prisoners so they could drink, too. As long as they cooperated no one was harmed, but he tried to slip away to come for help. When they caught up with him they beat him and left him for dead."

"Is he well enough that he could show us which direction they went?" Kandake asked.

"No," her father said. "The beating has blinded him."

"Then we will never see Alara again." Tabiry resumed her weeping.

"That will be quite enough," her mother said. "Your brother will be fine. Nubia will find a way to rescue him." She looked to her husband as if for assurance.

Kandake dropped her gaze to the floor. She knew what her father must say. There could be no formal rescue. Nubia was at war and needed every warrior—here. The fresh breeze of hope soured around them, wilting the newly kindled optimism. Worry's stale breath pressed in on the gathered family, once again.

"We will do the best we can," the king said. "Kashta is preparing a small party to find whatever trail may be left. We will decide what to do once we have more information."

# # # #

The next few days were harder for Kandake. Now she had news that her brother was alive, but there was nothing she could do to bring him home. She listened as her father and Uncle Dakká discussed Nubia and Alara.

"There has to be a way, Dakká," King Amani challenged his brother. "Find it."

"We are examining every option, My King," he said. Uncle Dakká spoke with Kashta in low tones. They reviewed the inlaid map of Nubia on the table with marks indicating the placement of companies of warriors around the kingdom, and the warrior roster.

Kandake scrutinized the expression on her uncle's face. She read the doubt in his eyes. She watched him scrub his forehead with the back of his hand. A gesture he often used when something worried him.

"Now that we have the skirmish at our northern border contained," Uncle Dakká said, "it may be possible to send a contingent of warriors to bring him home without weakening Nubia's position.

"That is promising." King Amani sat forward, his mood brighter, hope returning to his eyes. "How soon can they leave?"

"It will take some time to get reports from all of our outposts. Once I am assured that the boundaries of Nubia cannot be breached, it should not take long getting the warriors supplied and on their way."

"How long?" The king's voice held an edge tinged with impatience.

"My King," Uncle Dakká again rubbed his forehead. "The reports from our farthest outposts will take at least one week. And even then…."

Kandake heard and understood what her uncle left unsaid. She knew her father grasped the same understanding. He sagged against the back of his chair. She had never seen him in such a state. Her own feelings of defeat tugged at her.

Sending a party of warriors large enough to meet an unknown threat to secure her brother's safety would reduce Nubia's defenses. Her enemies could damage or possibly overtake her. And, if they waited for all of the reports, supposing they were favorable for a rescue attempt, it could be too late for Alara.

Who has him? Where are they taking him? What do they want? Kandake sorted through all of the information made available by her brother's servant. None of it helped. It did not tell her where Alara was being held or why.

Her eyes wandered over the faces of those around the table. Natasen's face was its usual stone, but she read through it easily enough. His eyes always gave him away. They smoldered with the same angry energy seething within her. The faces of Uncle Dakká and Kashta bore the same anger, but theirs was infused with worry.

Aunt Alodia's face was a mask of concern, but whatever else she was thinking or feeling was shielded from easy observation. Uncle Naqa mopped his brow with a square of weathered cloth while his eyes searched the room for answers. She wondered if he thought they were hidden in the darkened corners. Kandake discovered Tabiry's expression to be unusually open. It displayed anger and fear. Her eyes bore into Kandake's. They pleaded for action.

_30_

"I cannot believe they are not going to do anything," Tabiry said. "They cannot leave Alara with those people. He could die." She looked from Natasen to Kandake. When neither said a word, she pulled at Kandake's arm, "You are going to do something?"

"What is it you want me to do?" Kandake bit back. "I would love to say they are wrong, but they are not. If Father ordered warriors to rescue Alara now, it would put Nubia in jeopardy, especially since Assyria could be waiting outside our borders. We have to wait."

Sitting together on the ground, beyond the stables, Kandake grabbed what refuge she could in the company of her siblings. The weather was enjoyable— a day, bright with sunshine and refreshing breezes; even the flies left them alone. Kandake neither noticed nor cared. The storm that brewed within her caused her limbs to feel like weighted bags of sand.

"Wait? For what?" Tabiry demanded.

"Wait for the danger threatening Nubia to pass," Natasen said. "Wait for the timing to be right." He pulled his knife from its casing, shaved another spot on his forearm. Kandake noted that his arms were missing quite a bit of hair. Testing the edge of his blade in this way had become Natasen's standard since Alara had gone missing.

"You are scheduled to patrol the southern border in the next few days, right?" Tabiry asked her brother. "Once you are far enough south, what is there to stop you from heading east until you have found Alara?"

"No. A warrior does as he is ordered. Anything else would leave Nubia vulnerable," Natasen said, his expression severe.

"Alara is vulnerable!" Tabiry spat. "He is just as important as this kingdom."

"Yes, he is," Kandake said. "But he is not more important than this kingdom."

"And you said that you would be a warrior queen!" Tabiry dissolved into tears. She neither keened nor wailed. She wept without sound, but her body shuddered and shook.

Kandake watched her sister's grief. She felt her brother's frustration. Tabiry was right, something had to be done. But so were her father and uncle. Warriors could not be sent away from Nubia, not now, not when the kingdom needed them most.

She filled her hand with the dust and gravel they sat upon. As a distraction, she sorted the pebbles from the fine grit and grains of sand. The small stones were easy to separate. Dividing the grit from the dust was another matter. It blended too well.

An idea began to form in the small crevices of her mind. If there was a way to save Alara, it was here.

She stared at the handful of gravel, deciphering its secrets.

"What are you looking at?" Natasen asked. "What is in your hand?"

"Just dirt, but I think I may have found a way to help Alara," she answered.

"What is it? Let me see?" Tabiry asked, grabbing her sister's hand. She stared at the handful of gravel. "What do you see? How is dirt going to help Alara?"

"Not this." Kandake tipped her hand and poured its contents onto the ground. "It is what it made me think of." She turned to her brother. "Natasen, what is the greatest danger of a large unit of warriors leaving Nubia right now?"

"The enemy would see that a significant portion of our protection had left. They would probably attack not long after the warriors had gone." He stared at Kandake. His expression said he was trying to see where she was going.

"Right, but what if they see a young female leaving—alone?"

"They would likely ignore her." A grin played at the corners of his mouth. "I see where you are headed. Who would you get to go? Father would never allow you."

"He cannot forbid what he does not know." Kandake's mind was moving at the speed of a lioness on the scent of her prey. "I would have to put together a plan, supplies, and find the right moment to leave."

"You could do this? Do you think you could bring Alara home?" Tabiry's face swung from Kandake to

Natasen and back again. For the first time since Alara went missing, Kandake saw hope in her sister's eyes.

"You just tell me what you need, I will make sure you have it," Tabiry said.

A sharp nod of Natasen's head assured Kandake of her brother's pledge of assistance.

"Good," Kandake said, accepting their help. "I will let you know as soon as I think it through. But Natasen is right. If Father or Uncle Dakká find out, they will stop me. So we keep it between us."

As Kandake walked toward the palace with her brother and sister, she noticed that Natasen's steps had regained their usual buoyancy. Tabiry no longer seemed the fragile bird she had become. Kandake became aware of the brightness of the sun in a brilliant, blue sky, and enjoyed the Nile's gift of a cool, moist breeze moved across her shoulders for the first time in what felt like a very long while.

31

"You cannot go by yourself," Ezena said. "What if there is trouble? A band of warriors could help."

"That is the problem. There are not any available and if they were seen, it would mean trouble for the kingdom. Nubia would suffer because of it." Kandake had to make her friend understand what she must do. "And if they did not attack the kingdom, it is certain that they would tie the warriors up in battle. It is best I go alone."

"Why must it be you? Could not another lone warrior go?"

"Send someone else to do what I must?" Kandake shook her head. "Who would I send?"

"I could go in your place."

"No, this is something I have to do. Besides, your sister is due to give birth, soon. She needs you here."

"This is not her first birth and she does not need me. Our mother will be with her."

"The answer is still no," Kandake said. She added the same amount of force to the word she had often heard her grandmother use. Her friend's silence assured Kandake that she had made her point. *No one argues with Great Mother for very long.*

"What I need is a supply of arrows," Kandake told her friend. "We cannot take them from the stores. Our warriors will need those. Will you help me make more? Could you get Nateka to make the arrowheads for me?"

"Of course, but for the shafts, you need Amhara's help more than mine. He pulls the straightest ones."

"Do you think he would do it?" Kandake asked. She wanted the help, but she was reluctant to let too many people in on her secret. The more people who knew about her plan increased the chances of her father finding out. She was sure that would be the end of her intentions to help Alara.

"You know how he cares about you," Ezena grinned. "He could not deny his queen anything."

32

"I am telling you for the last time, Kandake," Amhara said, his voice rasping in whisper. He stuffed the remaining bundle of arrows into one of the holes they had dug. Kandake had buried her supplies beneath one of the large thorn bushes on the side of the palace. Because of its sizeable barbs, the scrub had been allowed to grow to sufficient height to discourage intruders from entering the windows. "You should let Ezena or me go with you."

"And I am telling you for the last time, Amhara. No." Kandake filled in the hole around her bundle. She spread the remaining sand and stubble to camouflage her cache of supplies. "If I go alone, I have a better chance of getting past the enemy."

"You are growing to be a stubborn woman." Amhara checked her work. He made sure there were no telltale signs of the small armory hidden beneath the soil and walked away in a huff.

Stubborn is only one way of looking at strength. Kandake knew Amhara meant well, he only wanted her to be safe, but she could not risk his life, or anyone else's, on what she was about to do. She watched the smooth contraction and release of the muscles in his back as he walked away.

As soon as I return, she thought, studying the bunch and flow of strength beneath Amhara's skin, *I will have that conversation with Mother about taking a suitor. And when he presents himself, there will be no argument from me.*

"Kandake," Natasen signaled to his sister as she entered the palace. "I leave on patrol in the morning. How are your plans going?"

"Fairly well," she said, her voice not more than a whisper. "I have just about everything I will need."

"Take this." He handed Kandake a small dagger. "I worked this one myself. The blade is hammered strong so it will not break. Its tang runs through the hilt for greater strength. It will hold its edge and never fail you. Wear it in a place it cannot be seen."

"Thank you." Kandake took the gift from her brother. She hefted it to get a feel of its weight and balance. She tucked it out of sight beneath her clothing.

"I wish I was going with you." He leaned forward and rested his forehead against his sister's. Kandake knew this gesture to mean her brother loved her very much. Pulling away, Natasen looked deeply into Kandake's eyes as if he were carving a memory into his mind. "Live strong, My Queen."

Natasen lowered himself to one knee. He bowed his head, honoring his sister. Kandake laid her hand on the back of his head showing him great favor. Natasen rose, turned away from his sister, and rushed into the night.

_33_

    Kandake tossed on her bed. Sleep eluded her. Swimming through her mind were all of the details of what she was taking on. Did she have the right supplies? Would she need more food? If she managed to leave the palace unseen, would the same hold true for leaving the kingdom?

    In the last few days she had gathered all of the weapons and supplies she believed she would need for her journey. To Kandake's surprise, Tabiry had been true to her word. She made sure Kandake had the extra dried meats and fruits for this undertaking, and not just travel rations, either. Tabiry had included a few fresh food items like dates and vegetables, grains for Strong Shadow, and even good bladders to carry fresh water in. The best of all was the package of medicines, herbs and bandages. With these she would be able to help Alara if he were injured.

    Tabiry had even managed to smile at Kandake on rare occasions. _I think she is crying less, too,_ Kandake mused.

    Still unable to sleep, she traded her bed for the windowsill. Pushing the window covering behind her back, she gazed out at the wide moon shining its face down at her.

"What if I cannot do this? What if I cannot find Alara? Fears and doubts filled Kandake's heart, bubbling up and boiling over until they replaced her conviction that this was the right thing for her to do. Her body shuddered at thoughts of what she might find. What she would be up against. *I cannot do this* screamed every portion of her—mind, body, spirit.

But what was the alternative? Alara would have to wait until her father and Uncle Dakká deemed it safe for a full complement of warriors to retrieve him. What if his captors were not willing to wait that long? What if they harmed him? What if...

The decision was already made for her. Not going after her brother was not a choice she or Alara could afford. Her brother was in jeopardy and she was the only one that could help. Kandake inhaled, filling her lungs to capacity. She let the breath out in a slow, smooth stream as she often did to settle herself for a difficult shot.

Her grandmother's words came rushing into her like much needed air.

"Great Mother is right," Kandake muttered into the night. "There is much to be done and I will see it through to the end."

Kandake left her perch and rearranged the window covering, blocking out the moon's light. She made her way through the darkness and lay down on her bed. "Alara has waited long enough. I will leave tomorrow after the palace has gone to sleep." Turning onto her side, sleep claimed her for its own.

34

Sliding over the windowsill of her bedroom, Kandake made her way from the palace to the first hiding place of her supplies. She wore her breastplate and riding cape. For stealth, her feet were clad in soft-soled sandals. Her bow and quiver of arrows hung at her back. Below her waist, her knife rode on her right hip and her sling pouch dangled from her left.

Kandake had decided a secretive exit would be best. She could have left in the daylight, but when she failed to return that night, a warrior would raise an alarm. She needed as much time as she could squeeze out before someone noticed she was gone. Should her absence be noticed before she was far enough away, a warrior would be dispatched, either by her father or Uncle Dakká, to bring her back.

Taken from one of the holes beneath the thorn bushes, Kandake slung the bag of foodstuffs and medicines over her shoulder and made her way to her cache of weapons. Amhara was waiting for her outfitted in the same manner—bow and filled quiver, a knife at one hip, and his sling pouch hanging from the other.

"I have decided that you cannot go alone," he said, taking one of the bags from her. "So I am going with you."

"You may go with me as far as the stables," Kandake said. Her heart wanted him to go with her, but she could not lead him into unknown dangers. "The stables and no farther." She tried for her grandmother's assertiveness, knowing all the while that she wanted him to come along.

Amhara did not argue. He only slipped another of her bundles onto his shoulder and walked in silence. When they reached the stables, Ezena was waiting.

"What is he doing here?" Ezena asked Kandake.

"He thought he was going with me, but I have corrected that notion."

"Good," Ezena said, adjusting the fall of her bow. "I am going with you. After all, if you are seen alone with him at night, it would attract too much attention."

"You are not going, Ezena, I am." Amhara glared at his cousin.

She gave him the same.

"Listen," Kandake said, stepping between them. "Neither of you is going. I am going alone. I cannot risk either of you getting hurt or worse."

Kandake walked into the stables and made her way to Strong Shadow's ample stall. Tied up next to her horse were Ezena's and Amhara's.

"This will not change my mind," Kandake said, staring at the three horses saddled and prepared to travel. She moved to her horse and began tying on and draping her supplies over the animal's back.

"I did not do this," Amhara said.

"Neither did I," Ezena shrugged her shoulders.

"Well, if you two did not, who did?" Kandake asked, looking from one friend to the other. "Who else knows about this?"

"I do not know, but the horses are not the only things that were brought here." Ezena pointed to the far side of the stall. Piled against it were sacks and bundles bulging their contents.

The three walked over to where the collection lay. Kandake opened the first one. It contained two riding capes, four fresh bowstrings, ropes, and varying lengths of leather straps. The package Amhara opened was filled with arrows and sling stones. Ezena's was filled with foodstuffs, more medicine and bandages, and healing herbs.

"Who could have put all of this here?" Ezena asked. "Who knows you are leaving?"

"Tabiry and Natasen are the only ones I told, other than the two of you." Kandake wondered if her sister would have been able to arrange all of these extra items. "She was supposed to get the supplies I would need, but all of this," she waved her in the direction of the sacks of supplies, "is beyond her."

"Do you think Natasen put this together?" Ezena asked, staring in wonderment at the amount and assortment of provisions piled and waiting for them.

"I do not believe so," Kandake said. "He could get the weapons, but not the medicines."

"Whoever put it together," Amhara said, "we will thank them when we get back. Right now, we need to get it all loaded."

Kandake started to renew her argument against her friends' accompaniment, but she surrendered, allowing herself to be persuaded. She knew she could use their help and their company would be welcome.

After they had tied the last of the bundles to the horses, Kandake swung up into Strong Shadow's saddle. When she mounted, she noticed a small pouch tied to the bronze ring of a saddle strap. She hefted it. Its weight made her curious to know what was inside.

Opening the parcel, she discovered several heavy rings of gold bound together with threads of silver, a small collection of gemstones including a lapis stone bearing the marks of the king of Nubia. The blue stone, bearing the mark that signified her father's rule, would be available should she need proof that she represented Nubia or if the possibility of an alliance arose. A folded parchment lay at the bottom of the bag. She unfolded the sheet, smoothed it out against her thigh, and began reading.

"What is it?" Ezena asked, squinting at the page from her horse's back.

"It is a copy of the report Kashta brought to Father. He describes his search using the information he got from Alara's servant." She turned the page over. "This is the map that goes with it. It shows the places he found clues to the direction in which they might have taken my brother."

Tears flooded her eyes. It was clear these things could not have come from Natasen or Tabiry. It would take someone with more power than they had to put something together like this. But who? Mother? Father? Great Mother? One of her uncles? Could it have been Aunt Alodia? It did not matter where the help was coming from. Someone was helping her to do what was needed and she was grateful.

She refolded the sheet, blinked away her tears, and nudged Strong Shadow forward. "We go."

They took the long way around, traveling behind the stables, moving in the shadows at the back of the warrior compound. Once they got beyond it they dismounted, walking their horses past the palace. Several times Kandake thought warriors had seen her small party. She expected someone to stop them. It was odd. No challenge came. In fact, no one appeared to notice them as they made their way to the edge of the palace courtyard.

"We will remount here. If we get stopped," Kandake whispered, "let me do the talking. If they attempt to bar our way, I can order them to let us pass. Unless my father has given them specific instructions to stop me, they have to let us go through."

It took the trio most of the night before they reached the last outpost of Nubia's nearest border. Kandake and her friends passed through without challenge or notice.

"That was strange," Amhara said, his voice barely audible. "It is like they are making a point of ignoring us."

"That has to be it," Kandake said, her voice equally as low. "There is no way our warriors could not have noticed us. We need to cover as much ground as we can tonight. Tomorrow promises to be a long day."

Kandake and the others kneed their horses into a gallop. As they left Nubia behind, Kandake's mind raced to what lay ahead. Although she pushed forward with determination, a chill of apprehension lined her stomach. There was no going back, not without Alara.

35

Kandake's small band rode hard once they passed the last of Nubia's camps. No one attempted to stop them; neither were they pursued. With the moon's bright face lighting their way, they covered quite a bit of ground before resting.

Amhara laid out their blankets. He positioned them in a wheel, heads nearly touching, and faces watching all directions. There would be no fires on this trip; their presence could not be announced. With each member sitting on their cover, Kandake spread out the map for all to examine.

"I believe we are just beyond Alara's initial site," she said, taking her bearings from the landscape around them. "In the morning, we should continue heading east." Her finger traced a path to their next landmark.

"What are those markings?" Amhara asked, leaning over the map.

"That is where Senka found Alara's servant. From there, the map gives us one more help. After that we track the rest of the way."

"Do you think their traces will be very hard to find?" Ezena asked.

"Kashta says the attackers attempted to remove their marks, but if we look for large disturbances in the terrain, we should be able to find our way," Kandake answered through a huge yawn. "We move out at daybreak."

"I will take the first watch," Amhara said.

"Good, I will take the second one," Ezena volunteered.

"That leaves me for the last one," Kandake said. "I will have the horses ready and the morning's rations prepared when I wake you." Making sure she received a nod of agreement from the other two, she lay her head down. Thoughts of Alara waiting for her lulled her to sleep.

The sky opened with the sun's first rays shining, Kandake accepted its greeting. She and her friends were already making their way to the map's next landmark.

Amhara dismounted and searched the ground. Squatting low, he scrutinized the earth for telltale marks that would give the trio the information they needed for their quest. He moved to a darkened area of soil.

"This is probably where they found your brother's servant." He took a pinch of the stained earth and brought it toward his nose. "It smells of blood."

Kandake walked a wide circle around where Amhara stood, examining the ground she trod. The area had been well-trampled. She read the signs of several horses and the footprints of those riding them.

"Kandake, come look at this," Ezena said. She had something in her hand, turning it over and over, examining every side.

"What is it?" she asked, approaching her friend.

"I am not sure. It is a stone, black as ebony with something carved into it." She offered it to Kandake.

"I have never seen these characters before," she said, tracing the etchings with her fingers. She examined the other side, a face with unfamiliar features stared back at her. "Can you identify it?" She handed it to Amhara.

"No, I do not know these markings. But I have heard of something like this." He turned it over in his hands. "I believe this emblem identifies the carrier as a ruler's representative."

"What ruler?" Ezena asked, peering over her cousin's shoulder. "How did it get here?"

"I do not know," Amhara answered, giving the stone back to Kandake. "Which way do we go from here?"

She tucked the piece into the pouch that held the gemstones and gold rings." According to the map, we have one more hard ride before we are on our own." Kandake showed the map to her friends before folding it and adding it to the pouch. "We will water the horses, have a small meal, and then ride."

Amhara poured fresh water from a bladder into oiled hides that took on the shape of bowls as they filled. He set one before each horse. Ezena rationed out dates, small onions, and dried meat into three portions. She handed one of these to each person and sat in the dust next to Kandake.

The farther they traveled from the Nile, the drier the air became. The sun was unrelenting; heat waves shimmered around them. Insects buzzed at their faces and exposed limbs, looking to drink from the beads of sweat now turning into small streams.

Kandake passed around a bladder of water, each drinking in turn. Rising from the dust, she pulled her cape from a bundle on Strong Shadow's back and covered herself. It offered some protection from the sun's attack. The band of friends swung to the backs of their horses and headed in the direction the map indicated. They pushed their animals hard, as far as they dared.

After covering some distance, the group slowed their mounts to a careful trot. Everyone focused on the ground as they moved ahead. Their change to an unhurried pace was as much to cool down their rides as to protect the animals' feet. Rocks jutting up unexpectedly, cracks in the crumbling ground, were a hazard for hooves. This was not the place for your horse to be injured or go lame. Without shelter and a supply of fresh water, survival here would be a very risky option.

As the sun slid across the sky to its nightly refuge, Kandake caught sight of the landmark on the map. Pointing out the location to Ezena and Amhara, they turned in that direction.

Reaching their destination, Kandake saw to the needs of their horses, Amhara took his turn at preparing their meal, and Ezena laid out their bedding for the night. Far outside the boundaries of Nubia, the darkening sky brought unwelcome questions to worry Kandake. They harassed like biting insects.

We have come so far, she thought, setting out water for each animal. *How much farther before we find him?* Kandake began wiping the sweat and dust from Strong Shadow's back and neck. Long, slow strokes accompanied her thoughts. *Who are these people and what do they want with my brother? If they have harmed him....* The horse snorted and stepped away from her emotion-fueled swiping. "I am sorry, boy." She patted his side in apology. "I am just a little worried."

She continued to give Strong Shadow comforting pats as she completed her task at a gentler pace. Kandake moved to Amhara's ride. He was not quite as tall as Strong Shadow, but every bit as sturdy. His coat bore the same rich, dark coloring. The horse remained calm under her experienced administrations.

What if Alara is hurt? How many will we have to fight to get him home? Can I really do this? The doubts stung her like the winged pests of the night air. She batted them away. For the insects, she snapped the soft hide she used to wipe the horses. She used warrior discipline for her thoughts. *I will do what must be done.*

36

Stretched out on her covers, Kandake was awakened by the sound of rock striking rock. She pretended to scratch her nose in her sleep. She let her arm fall just above her braids. With her fingers, she touched Ezena's head. She trusted that Ezena would understand her signal. Amhara had the watch; she was sure he saw what was happening.

In the darkness, a rough hand encircled Kandake's left ankle and yanked. The intention of the intruder may have been to frighten, but it spurred her into action. Using the force of her leg being dragged, Kandake countered it, pulling herself into a seated position. Her knife was at the intruder's throat. Amhara straddled him with an arrow nocked, pointing at the man's back.

The attacker's wide, frightened eyes shone in the dark. He fumbled for something within his robes. Ezena grabbed his arm, preventing his movement.

As a team, the friends lifted the man to his feet. With Kandake and Ezena covering him, Amhara peered into the darkness, prepared to greet any other visitors. Kandake lowered her knife and stepped away.

Ezena maintained her grasp of his arm, but moved behind him and pressed her knifepoint to his back.

"Who are you?" Kandake spoke into her attacker's face. "Why are you here?" He said nothing, eyes staring at her. Ezena pressed the point of her blade into his back, nicking his skin. He groaned in response.

"I said, who are you?" Kandake spoke threw clenched teeth. Her anger kept in control only with great effort. The intruder attempted to answer, but his apparent fear only allowed for stammered speech.

At Kandake's signal, Ezena released the pressure of her blade in his back, but held onto his arm. Her knifepoint remained snagged in his clothing. This way she kept him aware that the danger was not far away.

Swallowing several times, the man's Adam's apple bobbed and danced. He wet his lips and exploded into several syllables of unintelligible speech.

"What did he say?" Amhara called over his shoulder. "Can you understand him?"

"No," Kandake said, keeping her eyes on the intruder. "But one of the words sounds like Nubia." Focusing on his eyes, she asked, "What did you say?"

He repeated the words, but at a much slower pace. Kandake was sure he said something about Nubia. His pronunciation of the kingdom's name was mangled by his accent, but she was certain he had said it.

"What about Nubia? What are you saying?"

With his free hand, he pointed to an area of his clothing near the place where Ezena clasped his other.

Kandake signaled and Ezena released his arm, but increased her knife's pressure.

Using slow and deliberate movement, the man slid his hand into an inner pocket. After some fishing within, he removed it with the same unhurried care. He held out a closed fist to Kandake. She extended an open palm beneath it. The intruder let what he held fall into her waiting hand. A small, bronze bell rolled into Kandake's palm.

"Alara help," he said, pointing to the bell.

"Alara?" Kandake grabbed the front of the man's garment. "What do you know about Alara?" Hope and anguish fought for position within her.

The man jabbered. He made sounds that slammed together making no sense to anyone. His speech ended with his slapping his chest, pointing in the direction from which the friends had come. He repeated the words, "Nubia, Alara, help."

"I think he is trying to tell us that he is going to Nubia to get help for your brother," Amhara said.

"You know where my brother is?" Kandake asked, eagerness winning out over anxiety. "Where is he? Can you take us to him?" At the man's blank stare, Kandake started again, this time remembering he likely could not understand her words, either.

"Alara," she said, exposing the bell in her hand. "You know Alara?" she asked him, pointing first to him and then to the small bronze piece she held.

He responded with more gibberish, nodding his head. This time he pointed to himself, then to Kandake's hand saying, "Alara."

At a gesture from Kandake, Ezena released him. Amhara came to stand next to her. Kandake offered the strange man a drink of water. When he had swallowed several mouthfuls, she offered him food. He declined.

Kandake indicated the bit of metal in her hand and asked, "Alara, where?" She turned in a small circle with her hand extended, hoping he would understand.

He repeated her brother's name and pointed northeast.

"Show me," she said, pulling on his garment and facing the direction he indicated.

"Alara," he repeated, shaking his head in the negative. He spoke more of the gibberish. He slapped his chest and then turned toward Nubia, taking a few demonstrative steps.

Kandake tried again to get him to show them where to find her brother. Again he refused, jabbering and swinging his arm, beckoning them to go with him to Nubia. After the third attempt he pointed at each of them and held up three fingers. He picked up two stones from the ground, one smaller and sharper, and made scratches on the larger stone. He held up three fingers again, handed Kandake the scratched stone, and pointed in the direction of Alara.

Amhara took the stone from Kandake and counted the scratches. "He is saying that there are twenty-five men holding Alara. Those odds are not the best, but it is possible."

Kandake was torn. She knew the man had a point. With a full complement of Nubian warriors, the twenty-five men holding her brother did not stand a chance. If she left now, riding hard, she could bring back warriors that would be sure to free her brother. She stared at the ground, deciding what to do.

The warriors were not available. They were needed to protect Nubia. It had to be her. There was no other help. If Alara is to be freed, she would have to save him.

"Show me Alara," Kandake said. She pointed to the ground and then pointed to her brother's bell. The man understood. He bent down and began scratching directions in the loose dirt. After several tries and much pantomiming, the three had a general understanding of how to find the camp where Alara was being held.

Kandake reached down and snapped one of the fine golden bells from the circle around her ankle. This she joined with her brother's bell and pressed them into the man's hand. She pointed to the bronze bell and said her brother's name. She pointed to the golden one, then to herself and said, "Kandake."

She closed his fingers over them, touched his chest, and gave him what she hoped was a questioning look. After a short spate of gibberish the man said what sounded like 'Jarn' while tapping his chest with vigor.

He pointed to the bells in his hand he said, "Alara, Kandake." He pointed to himself and repeated, "Jarn."

"Jarn," Kandake said, tasting the strange name. "You go to Nubia," she told him, urging the man in the general direction of her home. At her instruction, Amhara gave him a bladder of water and a small parcel of food. Mounting their horses, the three rode to find her brother.

37

Riding through the night and into the morning, Kandake, Ezena, and Amhara came to the ridge that Jarn had indicated. Tying their horses some distance from the edge, Kandake and her friends inched on their bellies until they could see over it.

The camp lay below them in a small gorge protected on two sides by high walls. The view showed them two ways into the camp. To the south, the opening was wide and straight enough for easy access. At least four or five men, riding abreast, could enter and exit with ease. To the north, the opening was narrow and steep, turning on itself several times. Its width would allow for maybe two horses, if they were small.

Four shelters with walls of animal skins stood together in a curving line; each facing the large fire ring in front of them. Several carcasses, speared on raised rods, roasted over the fire.

Kandake could see only a few men milling around. The number of horses corralled at the far side of the camp indicated that there were many more riders inside.

At the northern end of the encampment, a small pen held more than a few goats. This was no makeshift campsite to be set up at dusk and struck at dawn. Everything about it indicated it had been here for a while and gave no sign that it would be dismantled any time soon. The number of animals kept in the pen made that point quite clear.

The trio moved away from the rim of the gorge with the same stealth they had used to approach it. At a safe distance, they sat together in the shade of a large group of rocks.

"I cannot tell how many men are actually down there," Amhara said after a long pull on the bladder of water Ezena had passed him. "We cannot go in until we know the number we will be facing."

"There is that," Kandake said, taking a turn sucking the refreshing liquid, "and the problem that we cannot see where they are holding Alara."

"We need to get in there," Ezena said. "One of us could go in tonight."

Kandake looked to the sky, and judging from the position of the sun she said, "It is only late morning. I do not think we can wait. The longer we are here, the more water we use. We gave Jarn a full bladder. There is just enough for us to make it back, but it will be close. And adding Alara and his party...," she shrugged. "We need to get moving as soon as we can. We have no idea what they are going through down there."

Kandake brooded over their next move. *Can Alara afford the time it will take for us to wait for nightfall to gather the information we need? Without it, we cannot hope to put together a workable plan. We need to know what we are facing.*

Nearby sounds broke into Kandake's thoughts. She spied Amhara pulling something from the pack on his horse. Shaking it out, he brought the item to where she was sitting. He spread the length of fabric over his lap as he sat. Its coloring was mottled. In scattered places, it matched the earth beneath them; in others, its shading shifted from darker to lighter. Lengths of string dotted its surface in a disorganized fashion.

"What is that?" Kandake asked.

"This is how a warrior can be invisible in plain sight. I brought it case I needed to disappear," he said, smiling. "With this we do not have to wait for the cover of night to get what we need."

"But you have just learned that skill," Ezena said. "You have not mastered it yet. They will see you."

"Not if I am careful, move at a very slow pace, and stay in the shadows."

Amhara studied the terrain around them as he plucked bits of dried grass, rock, and other vegetation that grew there. Once he had gathered a suitable pile of debris, he began to tie it onto the fabric. Gradually, it started to take on the look of the land upon which they sat. After tying the last fragments, Amhara spread it out on the ground and covered it with dirt.

Taking care not to disturb the dust he had added, he slipped his arms through the loops on the underside. He covered his head and tied it at his neck. He took a few short steps forward and a length of the cover trailed behind him.

"How do I look?" Amhara asked. He grinned at them like a mischievous little boy.

"Strange," Kandake said. "How do you suppose this makes you invisible?"

"I can show you. You and Ezena have to close your eyes. By the time you count to twenty, I will be hidden."

Kandake and Ezena closed their eyes and began their count in a cadence that reminded Kandake of childhood games. Reaching twenty, they opened their eyes and scoured the area. Kandake focused. She examined every inch of ground around them, but it all looked the same. She picked up a few small rocks and threw them where she thought Amhara was hiding. Each stone landed with the thud of hitting solid ground. She looked to Ezena to see if she had spotted him.

"He must have left the area," Ezena said.

"It is not a true evaluation if you leave the section you were supposed to hide in," Kandake called reminding him of the boundaries he was supposed to conceal himself in.

"I have not left," he said. Amhara uncovered himself less than two arm's lengths to their right. He had blended his cloaked body with a small rise in the ground.

"I could not see you at all. This could work," Kandake said, her voice filled with amazement. "You could get in and out without them catching a glimpse of you. How much time do you think it will take you to do it?"

"It will take me the rest of the day and well into the evening," he said. "I will come in from the last bend in the northern entrance and start my crawl there. Because I cannot be in constant motion, it will take me considerable time. If I slide around the goat pen toward the rear of the shelters, I can check each one. That will give us a better idea of how many we face and locate Alara and the others."

"Kandake and I will cover you from the rim over there," Ezena said, her voice rang with respect for his accomplishment. She pointed to the spot where they had watched the camp.

"We should be able to target any threat to you," Kandake said. "But do not take any chances. If someone sees you, get up and run. We will make sure they do not get close enough to hurt you." Her voice held the sharp edge of command, but it was laced with an undercurrent of concern.

"They will not see me, my queen." Amhara winked, dipped a quick knee, and headed for the northern pass.

_38_

Kandake and Ezena pulled the bows from their bundles. The young women carried two sheaves of arrows in addition to their full quivers. They draped their capes about them to protect their skin from the sun's blistering rays and crawled to the rim's edge to watch.

As they lay there, they placed their supply of arrows within easy reach and laid one arrow across each of their bows. Kandake scoured the path leading into the camp, trying to find any sign of Amhara. She satisfied herself with the knowledge that if she could not pick him out from the terrain with her bird's-eye view, then it was likely that neither could the men holding her brother.

She changed her attention to the goings-on within the camp. Several men tended the meat roasting over the fire. Others brushed the horses and provided water for them. One man fed the goats.

The wait was grueling. She had no way of knowing just where Amhara was. The thought that at any moment one of these men could spot him creeping into the camp was unnerving.

Ezena touched Kandake's arm and indicated the direction she should shift her attention. A man on horseback entered the camp from the southern path. A wedge of dust clouds followed close behind. His hasty dismount and his wild gestures had the look of frustration, if not anger. The men in the yard rushed toward him. Voices reached the rim in a mish-mash of sound. Unintelligible noise at this distance, but the rhythm made it clear these men were not speaking any language Kandake could recognize. The rider broke through the engulfing mass, making his way toward the second shelter from him. Those who had gathered returned to their interrupted chores.

"What do you suppose that was about?" Kandake whispered, rolling onto her back so that her voice would not carry to the men below.

"I am not sure," Ezena said, her voice no louder than Kandake's, lying on her back as well. "I hope whatever that is about has nothing to do with Amhara."

"He came from the opposite direction. It must be something else."

Kandake returned to her belly and resumed her watch. A moment later, a well-built man exited the shelter and strode to the clearing near the fire ring. His bearing, and the way the others responded to him, named him as a man of some ranking. He approached several men and each left him with purpose marking their strides.

Soon after, men were brought from the second to the last shelter and lined up before him. Kandake assumed these were their prisoners. Their hands were tied in front of them.

She searched the line-up of captives until she found her brother. There he stood, his clothes dirty and torn. The ranked man must have said something because she saw her brother's head snap up from its lowered position. This man of rank delivered her brother a blow across his face. Alara stumbled backwards from the force.

In rapid response, Kandake raised her bow, lined up the point of her arrow on the man's head, and pulled her bowstring back its absolute limit. Ezena's hand covered hers, preventing her arrow's release. This she followed with an urgent hand sign.

Filling her lungs to capacity, Kandake emptied them in a slow discharge that helped her to achieve the calm her friend's signal implored.

Kandake's eyes fastened onto her target. *Ezena is right, now is not the time. I will wait. Then you will receive what your hitting my brother has earned you. And I will do the paying.*

39

The prisoners were returned to the shelter. Kandake willed Alara to hold on. She shifted her eyes back to the other end of the camp and searched the ground for any sign of Amhara.

Ezena tapped her arm and pointed. Kandake looked. At the back of the shelter her brother just entered, there was a wrinkle in the hide that served as its rear wall. Kandake could think of no reason for the hide to be gathered like that unless it was caused by their friend. Sometime later there was another pleat at the back of the next shelter. It remained for a while then disappeared. These were the only indications they had that Amhara was in the camp below.

Kandake and Ezena watched and waited until long after nightfall. There was no way of knowing where their companion was, or what progress he had made.

"What is so interesting down there?" Amhara's voice whispered at their backs. The two slid away from the rim without making a sound. At a safe distance from the edge, they stood and joined Amhara at their small campsite.

189

"What did you find out?" Kandake asked. Her voice betrayed the relief she felt at his safe return.

"There are a few more than twenty-five men down there," Amhara said around a mouthful of meat and bitter herbs. He took a pull on a bladder of water, careful to swish it around his mouth before swallowing. Dirt and gravel encrusted his face and arms.

"There are too many for us in a direct challenge," Ezena said. "We need a way to cut their numbers."

"If I got in once, I can get in again," Amhara said. "Once inside I can begin to thin them out."

"No," Kandake argued. "That will only work for a few of them. And there you would be outnumbered and out maneuvered. If you are killed, there would only be two of us to face the rest."

"What if we got most of them to leave the camp?" Ezena asked. "Then we could handle what was left."

"That is a better idea, but how do we get them to leave?" Kandake asked. She and her friends sat pondering the possibilities. Ideas were bounced around, yet each was flawed in a way that would leave at least one of them vulnerable.

"If their horses were run out," Amhara said. "It would take more than a few to recapture them and return their mounts to the pen."

"You cannot take all of the horses," Ezena said. "They would use what was left to come after you. Then they would have you and their mounts. What is more, the horses are at the back of the camp. Taking them through the center would have everyone after you before you got very far."

"What if we used the back entrance?" Amhara said.

"It is too narrow to get that many horses away with any speed," Ezena said. "They will only catch up with you."

"Not if they are under attack," Kandake said. "Amhara, describe the northern passage for me."

Amhara illustrated it using a stick, carving into the earth. He explained the places where the pathway twisted or where steep ridges gnawed away at its edges. He used pebbles to indicate the bushes and large rocks along the way. Kandake attended to every word. She asked for clarification as she felt the ideas for a plan unfold in her mind.

"I think we can do it," she said. "First, Ezena and I will need to place ourselves—here and here." She pointed to where the passage made sharp turns with enough cover to hide them from easy view.

"Then, Amhara, you sneak in. Lead out as many horses as you can, using the northern route."

"They will hear the horses stirring," Ezena said, still concerned.

"I am counting on that," Kandake answered. "Amhara, you will lead the horses out at as fast a pace as you can manage, keeping as many with you as possible. Those men down there will just be waking up and follow as soon as they make sense of the situation. Then, you ride all the way around to the southern entrance." Amhara nodded his head in understanding.

"Ezena, you will take the bend farthest away from the camp's entrance." Kandake placed a twig where she intended for her to hide. "Wait for the last riderless horse to pass you. You attack the riders as they pursue Amhara. I will not engage them until I see that they have committed themselves to fighting you. I will target the others as they come near me. Some of those responding to you will turn to shoot at me. I will get as many as I can. Together we should be able to cull out enough of them, making their numbers more manageable.

"When you are able, join me. We will harry them all the way back. I am hopeful that we disable a few more. Amhara will meet us from the other direction. That puts the three of us in the camp to fight and confuse them. We should be able to control what is left. We take Alara and the others home after I repay a particular debt."

The trio walked through Kandake's plan several times making sure each understood their part. After they had eaten the best meal they could in a cold camp, Kandake gave her final instruction. "We will take all of the arrows with us in the morning. We can return later for the rest of our supplies. We leave an hour before daybreak."

Stretching out for the night, Kandake reviewed the details of the plan.

What if I cannot do this? What if they kill us first? When the bandits attacked the caravan it took eight warriors to handle that many, and four of them had senior rank.

Doubt shook her. Fear lay in an icy ball at the bottom of her stomach. The two emotions wrapped themselves around her and began to squeeze.

Kandake took a deep breath, then another. She forced every muscle in her body to calm.

You wanted to be Prime. This is what you would have faced, she told herself. *Alara is depending on you.* She replayed the scene of her brother being struck in the face. Y*ou saw what that man did to him and there could be more. It is up to you. There is no one else.*

She placed all the details of the man who struck Alara firmly in her mind. She focused on the task of getting through the camp to reach him. Calm and determination returned to her.

And this is where I repay you for daring to hit my brother. Kandake smiled into the darkness, turned over, and went to sleep.

40

Kandake waited behind a group of large rocks at the first bend in the passage. Her riding cape protected her skin from the heat of the sun. It also allowed her to blend with her surroundings. She kept her movement to a minimum which prevented the fine dust at her feet from giving away her position. She made sure all of her arrows were within easy reach and checked that their flights were undamaged.

Time passed at the pace of a lazy serpent. Kandake shifted her position, giving her tired muscles some relief. *I wonder how far Amhara has gotten. It has been a long time,* she mused. *What if they see him sneaking into their camp? Then what?* She made another shift and felt the rumble through the ground seconds before she heard it.

Kandake crawled to the limit of her cover and got a glimpse of movement coming in her direction. Ducking back into hiding, she pressed her face to the narrow space between the boulders and saw multiple horses' legs passing in front of her. The waiting and not knowing what was happening was more than her nerves could tolerate. She secured the hood of her cape on her head and peeked over the top edge of the rocks that concealed her.

She caught sight of Amhara on the back of one of the camp's horses, riding in the middle of the swift-moving line of the herd. The pace of Kandake's heart slowed to a more normal rhythm. Something whizzed above her head. It thunked into the trunk of a nearby tree. An arrow. They were shooting at Amhara!

In less than the time it takes to think about her response, Kandake had an arrow nocked to her bow. She forced the plan into her mind. *Wait until they have passed,* she coached herself. *Give them time to reach Ezena.* She muttered a slow count to twenty-five. At twenty-six Kandake was on her feet, flinging arrows, taking only the time needed to nock them to her bowstring.

Her first arrows dropped two of the men before they realized they were being fired upon. But that did not last for more than a few seconds. One of them caught sight of her and sent arrows in her direction. She saw him change his course and ride toward her. He indicated to the others where she was. Several of them attempted to turn their horses on the trail to face her, but the pathway was too narrow for more than one to complete the maneuver at a time. Its soft steep sides and sharp rocks made leaving the route dangerous.

Kandake used the time to abandon her position and run for Strong Shadow hiding in a small copse nearby. Vaulting to his back, she turned him in the direction of the path and kneed him into action. She quick-marched her horse along the slender shelf she had been using. Strong Shadow bounded over the rocks that had concealed Kandake and landed on the path just as Ezena approached from her position farther up. Together, Kandake and her friend used their rapid fire to thin the number of attackers and send the men back the way they had come. The young women maintained their pressure on their adversaries until they all retreated.

Once inside the campsite, the men reversed their horses and blocked Kandake's and Ezena's path. Several men with long poles surrounded them, whacking their horses' legs. Ezena's horse stumbled. Kandake saw her friend struggle to maintain her seat as she pushed forward into the attacking swarm determined to grab her. Kandake watched as the horse attempted to shy away from its attackers, but Ezena leaned toward her horse's neck, further urging him forward.

They were surrounded. The men pressed in on them. At such close range, Kandake's bow was rendered ineffective. Instead, she used the weapon to hit her attackers in their faces and on their heads as hard as she could. She needed to do something, anything to get them to stop hitting Strong Shadow's legs.

Kandake watched as many hands dragged Ezena from her horse. Something caused Strong Shadow to stumble and shift his balance. The horse's movement loosened Kandake's seat, leaving her vulnerable to the men who snatched at her. Pulled from her horse's back, she hit the ground with a thud. The men pounced. Kandake was tied and dragged in front of the large fire ring. They dumped her next to a similarly bound Amhara. Ezena was on his other side in the same condition.

Those who dragged Kandake came within striking distance of Amhara. He thrashed about until he connected with the ankle of one of the men. Kandake's friend was rewarded with a rain of kicks and jabs with the horse poles for his efforts.

The attack on her friend enraged Kandake. She scooted and twisted until she was close enough to strike. One of the men pulled back his leg to deliver Amhara a brutal kick to his midsection. Kandake lifted her bound feet. She mule-kicked the man on the back of his supporting leg, below the knee. The blow knocked him off his feet. His buttocks hit the ground hard enough to raise dust. The other men snickered at him as he sat in the dirt.

He climbed to his feet and prepared to give Kandake what he had planned for Amhara. She braced herself for the strike that was certain to be more than a little painful. A bark of command from somewhere behind them froze the man's leg mid-swing.

"Just because this woman chooses to carry the weapons of a man," the voice said in her language, though heavily accented, "we do not treat her like one." He squatted near Kandake's head. His mirthless grin split his face. From where he had crouched, he turned his face toward a large man spitting angry words, pointing at the bound trio of young Nubians.

"Shen says, you and your friends killed four of my men and injured three others. He demands that I give you to them to return the favor.

The large man called Shen rattled off another spate of angry words, spittle flying as he spoke.

"He says that it is his right to have you. The men you killed were within his command."

Fear gripped Kandake's heart. Trussed up like this they could not defend themselves.

I cannot die here, her mind screamed. *What about Alara? Have I come this far for Nubia to lose two of my father's children, or two of my friends?*

Kandake reached within her soul, searching for strength she was not sure she would find. She dragged to mind anything that would help. The faces of her family. The faces of the children she had played the pitching game with.

I am warrior strong. I will not fear what I have not seen. Great Mother is right, I will see this through to whatever end comes.

Kandake focused on the man squatting near her. Nose-to-nose with her was the face she had etched into her memory. She owed him a debt and she would live to see that it was paid in full.

41

Kandake and Ezena were yanked from the ground and taken, hobbled by the bindings around their ankles. Pushed through the opening of the second shelter, Kandake struggled to see what was happening to Amhara. Inside, she and her friend were forced to kneel upon the animal hides that covered the center of the shelter's dirt floor. The large man called Shen sneered, standing over them, waiting.

Kandake took in the furnishings surrounding her. The room of hide walls was dim, requiring time for her eyes to adjust. Weapons of varying sizes and styles hung from a crosspiece that supported the pavilion. At one end of the rough-hewn table in front of them set a plate of roasted meat and a pitcher. The aroma wafting from it was foul-smelling and uninviting. The other end was blanketed in maps and scrolls. In the far corner of the shelter lay a pile of furs that had the rumpled look of bedding. The whole place reeked of too many days of camping and not enough washing.

"Why do you think we have been brought in here?" Ezena asked, looking around her. The tension

Stephanie Jefferson

Kandake read in her friend's face matched what she felt. Kandake shrugged her shoulders in response as she studied the space.

"What shall I do with two beauties that come to steal my horses?" The voice came from behind them, entering the shelter. "I must decide."

He brought himself into their line of sight. The man called Shen saluted him, then growled something and left.

"He says I should kill you. What do you think I should do?" He chuckled without humor.

Kandake's will took on the quality of iron. *I may be afraid, but you will never know.* She determined to neither bend nor break in the presence of this man or her circumstances. She fixed her eyes on the wall opposite her as he spoke.

"I am Commander Pho," he said, striking a pose as if his name should have meaning to them. "I was told when I was given this assignment that this is a wild, uncultured land. So much so, that the women are allowed to do whatever they like. They steal horses and even carry a man's weapons, so it seems." He paced a circle around the hides where the two Nubians knelt. He examined them like animals on display.

"I have the power to keep you for myself or sell you to the highest bidder," he said, his expression menacing. "Or I could kill you as Shen suggests. Which shall I do?"

You really believe you have 'power' over the throne of Nubia? This man's audacity would fill an Egyptian barge. Kandake fumed. She was incredulous at his words. Rage shoved whatever fear she had felt

200

far away from her. *Keep me. Sell me. Who does this arrogant pig think he is? His best choice would be to kill me. If he does not, I will kill him. I am the future of Nubia!*

The commander strutted around the enclosure. Kandake signed for her friend to be ready. He clearly did not see the danger of turning his back upon two Nubian warriors. She stared toward the doorflap, wondered how long they would be left alone with him.

"There is no one to save you here," he said when she turned her face toward him. As if he read her mind, he added, "No one comes through that doorway unless I call." He smirked and then continued his speech.

"The idea of a woman carrying a man's weapons...," Commander Pho chuckled, shaking his head. "And these two are barely more than girls. Such ideas these uncivilized dogs have."

He returned to the spot where Kandake and Ezena knelt. Reaching down he cupped a hand beneath Ezena's chin. He tilted her face up for closer examination. Kandake saw the lines of Ezena's body sharpen with her friend's growing tension. *Get your hands off of her. I promise, you will pay for that.*

"Quite comely," he said, leaning down and turning her face from one side to the other. "I may have to keep you for myself." He turned to look at Kandake. "But your friend has too much defiance in her eyes. She will have to be sold." He released Ezena's face and shifted his weight to lift her to her feet.

Kandake struck. Her movement was quick and silent. In an instant she took advantage of the commander's leaning position. Using his own weight against him, she pushed him to the ground. His face smacked the dirt floor beneath it. His breath whooshed from his body, raising a cloud of fine dust. Kandake used that brief second to whip the knife Natasen had given her from its secret place. She sliced the leather thong that bound her hands. She shoved her knee into the middle of his back, grabbed a fistful of his hair, snatched his head back, and placed her brother's gift to the man's throat. It was a sure promise of death should he move or dare to whisper.

Ezena moved with the same speed as her friend. She stripped Commander Pho of the weapons he wore. Using his knife, she slashed her bonds and those that remained around Kandake's ankles.

Kandake bent low and growled into his ear. "You are very arrogant for such an ignorant man. A Nubian warrior is neither male nor female. They cannot be bought, sold, or kept like a possession. You may barter for our services, if we have a fond respect for you. And at this moment I find myself without either fondness or respect in regards to you."

Kandake had a choice to make. She could kill this man, retrieve her brother, and return to her home. This was a possibility that suited her. But would that suit the queen of Nubia? The lessons of Aunt Alodia flooded her mind. Whatever decision she made now, Nubia would have to live with forever. Her mind and heart were at war.

He is not worth saving. She had heard the low opinion he had of Nubia and what it represented. He dared to take her brother. He had beaten one of Alara's servants and left him for dead—a citizen of Nubia. And he had dared to strike Alara. She saw this with her own eyes. These were the things that commanded the warrior within.

Then Kandake remembered the long war between a divided Nubia that Aunt Alodia insisted she study. A war caused by misunderstanding. A war that had diminished Nubia's precious resources and strength. Was she ready to do this to her home? Was she prepared to start a war with a people she knew nothing about? This man's ignorance brought her to this place. Would her own ignorance take Nubia farther down this road? *Think Kandake. You are not just a warrior, you are the queen. Will his death benefit Nubia, or harm it?* She cautioned herself to make the wisest choice for the kingdom.

This time her mind won over her heart. Kandake drew in a calming breath. She would not allow her anger to turn her into what Tabiry feared—a reckless, angry warrior who would bring nothing but trouble for the kingdom of Nubia.

"Right now I am trying to decide if the disrespect you have shown my brother is worth your life."

"Kill me." The commander spat past her blade. "A future king who allows himself to be rescued by a girl who steals horses and a commander that allows himself to be captured by one, neither is worth saving. Your actions shame me. Taken by a girl. How can I command an army of the Sovereign if you are able to do this to me?"

The commander's words and their tenor of disgrace struck pity in Kandake's heart. Her anger dissolved. *Because a woman captures you, this would make you choose death?*

"How can you be this ignorant? You are a man, not a child. How could you have so much to learn?" With her friend now armed, Kandake knew she could hold him as long as she needed. She eased him into a seated posture, but kept the knife to his throat. She signaled Ezena that the two of them should trade places so that she could see his face.

Kandake checked her position. She made sure she could cover the entryway and that Ezena had control of the commander. "Because I am in no hurry," she continued. "I will take the time to teach you."

She shifted into a comfortable stance, one that allowed her to choose the level of force of her blow for uninvited guests. "You have been sorely misinformed about Nubia. You need to understand that anyone in Nubia, if willing to train and build their strength can become a warrior; man or woman. The power and skill of our warriors is well known. There is a good reason our bow is feared. This is who we are and what we are capable of. The next time you are tempted to think of us as girls—weak and frightened, you would do well to remember who we are—Nubia Warriors.

42

"In your ignorance you assume you hold the next ruler of Nubia in that other shelter," Kandake said, pointing northward. "You do not hold the future of Nubia. That kingdom's future is standing in front of you. Here. Now. Warrior strong." She had the pleasure of seeing the commander's eyes widen in shock and disbelief. "Yes, a girl. A mere woman, as you would say. *I* am Nubia's next ruler."

The commander's face displayed absolute skepticism. "You lie. He wears the bells of royalty on his ankle."

"Yes, he does," Kandake answered. Bending down, she unwrapped the leather covering she had tied around her leg. She revealed the circle of gold that rested at her ankle. Twisting her foot gave song to the golden bells she wore. "Alara is the king's son and he is my brother, but I will rule."

She watched the commander's face move through a series of emotions as he digested the information. "I have decided that it is in Nubia's best interest not to give you the death you deserve—at least, not at this moment.

"You call Nubia uncultured and uncivilized, yet it is you who wonders that a woman carries weapons." Kandake warmed to her subject. "In my kingdom, a woman is respected for the strength she is born with."

"What strength can a woman have?" His question was more scorn than inquiry. He shifted, brushing away a stone that had lodged itself beneath his buttocks. "She can hardly bear the pain of bringing her own children into the world."

Kandake lowered her head, shaking it at the man's lack of understanding. She wondered how a culture could be so very different than her own. But here was a man who thought of women as weak, incapable of wielding a weapon, let alone ruling a kingdom. Was there anything of value that could come from a place that threw away half of its resources? These people were in sorry need of understanding.

"A woman shouts challenge and encouragement to her child. She goads that new life into existence. This is not weakness. It is only the start of the work she will do ensuring that her young one will have the courage to face what will come in life."

Kandake scrutinized the changes of his face as he considered her words. She took care in selecting what she would tell him about her home. "Nubia is a place of rich culture and strength. Each generation gifts the new one with wisdom and power for their future. We prosper because we are strong. We utilize every resource; that includes our women. This produces a kingdom that is united; one that has the strength of all its citizens working together. Protecting this, Nubia will endure."

When he scoffed at her words, Kandake chose her next ones to bite his pride. "That is how mere 'girls' capture a great commander."

43

Kandake and the commander talked well into the late afternoon. Each time one of his men asked entry, Commander Pho sent him away without moving from Ezena's blade. He hung on every word she had to say about her home. He told her of his home and his culture. Each asked the other questions and received answers.

"I would like to see this Nubia," Commander Pho said, with yearning. "But we are enemies. It could never happen." He let his shoulder fall, saddened by what could never be.

Kandake heard the regret in his voice. She saw the wistful look in his eyes. After a long moment's consideration, she made up her mind. "Friends," she said, "just like enemies, are chosen.

"I would like to have something that is hanging on my horse," she said. "Would you have one of your men retrieve it?" She walked away from the position she had taken near the shelter's entryway. At her signal, Ezena stepped from the commander, beckoning for him to rise.

"I am offering you an opportunity to learn of Nubia. Betray it...." She left the threat hanging. Kandake returned his weapons and secreted hers within her clothing once more. She described to the commander what she wanted. She counted on the commander's curiosity to keep him from raising any alarm. He did not disappoint.

She and Ezena resumed their places on the floor covering, sitting as guests, not kneeling in submission.

Commander Pho walked to the entrance, drawing the flap aside. He snapped out an order. A short time later, one of his men brought him the small parcel. The man made as if to linger, but at the commander's nod he left them. Commander Pho handed the sack to Kandake. He joined them, sitting on the skin-covered area.

Widening the bag's opening, she spilled some of its contents onto the floor. Two rings of gold and several gemstones lay glittering on the animal hide beneath her. From the pile, she removed one gold ring and a large jewel.

The stone was a little larger than the tip of Kandake's thumb. It was rounded on top and flat on the bottom. It had the rich, deep color of the late-night sky over Nubia. Within its dark blue field sparkled multiple flecks of gold. The whole of the stone's surface glistened like the face of the great Nile. The flat side had markings carved into it. Here was the token of the throne of Nubia, the offer of alliance.

Kandake pulled her knife from within her clothing and dug a small hole into the ground just large enough to hold the stone. She fitted it into the space, flat side up. Using the point of her blade as a chisel and a rock as a hammer, she added two lines to the stone's surface. She blew tiny shards out of the crevices as she examined her work.

"If we are ever to be friends," she told the commander. "You must release my brother."

"I cannot," Commander Pho said. "That would take an order from my superior officer or my Sovereign's Emissary."

"Where are they?" Kandake asked. "I would like to speak with them."

"I am afraid that, too, will be impossible. They were killed after we crossed the sea of sand."

"Surely there is someone assigned to act as their secondary if something happened to them?" Kandake said through clenched teeth, her patience reaching its limit. "Who would that be?"

"That would be me," Commander Pho said. His brows furrowed, forehead wrinkled.

"Then release my brother." Exasperated by what seemed to be his effort to set her chasing the wind, Kandake's voice bore the ring of command. All that was missing was her father's characteristic bellow.

"Princess, it is not within my power. If I release your brother without the authority, my Sovereign would consider me a traitor. I would be killed on sight. I could never go home again."

"But you said that you are the Second." She held onto her anger, but just barely. "Does not that give you the authority?"

"It is not that simple," he said. "I have the rank, but without the...." He flapped his hands in the air as if searching for an elusive word.

Kandake waited as he hunted for it.

At a loss, he gave up and continued. "It is a thing that represents the Sovereign's word. It is passed throughout all generations from our ancient one to now. The Emissary carries this stone of the ancestors. When he and my superior died, it should have passed to me. But it was lost."

Commander Pho shook his head as he studied the handful of gravel he picked up as he spoke. He flung it from him. "Without the stone, I lack the authority." Defeat scrawled itself all over him. He kept his gaze toward the floor as he continued.

"At first we thought your brother's party had attacked the Emissary and had taken it. We assumed the king of Nubia would want the powerful piece and demand something of our Sovereign. When we realized our mistake, it was too late. Now, without that piece, to release your brother would be seen as an act of disloyalty and treachery against the Sovereign."

"What does this 'piece' look like?" Kandake asked.

"It is a dark, iron stone. About the size of a large man fist, but it is flat and round. One side bears the likeness of the Sovereign's ancestor. It gives him the right to rule. The other side has the marks of the Sovereign."

As the commander spoke, Kandake thought of the stone Ezena had found in a field just beyond Alara's hunting site. She and Ezena exchanged glances. Ezena shrugged.

"Could this be it?" Kandake said, reaching into the sack and removing the stone. She offered it for his examination.

Commander Pho stared at the object Kandake held. His eyes widened in a face that was devoid of emotion. His eyes flicked from the piece, to Kandake's face, then back to what she held.

"If this is the valuable symbol you seek," Kandake said, "I have no desire to withhold it. If I return it, I do so as a friend, not as ransom for my brother." She lifted her chin. She took on the posture of a proud queen. "Nubians cannot be bought back like chattel. I would return this as a gift to a friend, the beginning of an alliance between our kingdoms."

Rising to his feet, Commander Pho pulled a measure of fine cloth from a pouch tied about his waist. With the fabric as a barrier, he lifted the stone from Kandake's hand. He wrapped it and tied a series of intricate knots securing it, mumbling and nodding as he went. When he finished, the parcel reminded Kandake of the beautiful pillows decorating her grandmother's rooms. Commander Pho bowed to the stone and placed it inside the smallish bag.

"You continue to shame me," he said. "We accused your brother of attacking the Emissary. We thought he had stolen the Sovereign's authority for the Nubian ruler to hold as ransom for an alliance or as treasure. Yet, you return it to me while I still hold your brother captive.

"Such honor is a rare thing for a queen or a warrior. It is clear that you are both."

_44_

"Let there be no misunderstanding," Kandake said. Her voice held the crisp ring of authority. "You will release Alara and all who are of Nubia." She stood and faced Commander Pho. Strength and resolve radiated from her. "As an act of friendship toward you and your Sovereign, I have returned what belongs to you. I expect and will accept nothing less."

His eyes raked the ground at his feet. Kandake watched the man before her struggle with his pride and culture. Would he betray her trust? As an act of honor she had given him the only thing she had to bargain with.

He raised his head, locked eyes with her. Kandake held his gaze. His was fierce, searching. She was reminded of Uncle Dakká's scrutiny. She had endured her uncle's inspections and prevailed. She would stand under this one. His eyes marked his decision.

"Would you walk with me, outside?" he said, executing a bow that was low to the ground. He walked to the entryway, careful not to give Kandake the disrespect of his back. He held the flap for her to walk through before him. The commander stepped through the opening behind Kandake and held it for Ezena.

Outside the hide shelter, the commander shouted an order. His men's response was immediate. They formed themselves in three even lines of six men with one standing slightly apart from the group. It was the one the commander called Shen. This position indicated that he held rank.

After they had lined up, Commander Pho shouted another order. It sent two of his men scurrying toward the shelter where Kandake believed Alara was being held. They returned with Alara, his hunting party, and a much-bruised Amhara. Each was bound at his hands and ankles.

The sight of her friend's condition rekindled the rage she felt about the same treatment of her brother. Kandake held her tongue and schooled her face to a careful neutral.

You people make it very difficult to hold back the warrior within me. Thoughts of repayment roiled inside her. She struggled to keep her hand from seeking the blade she kept next to her skin.

Kandake locked eyes with Amhara. A slight tilt of her head to the side silently asked the question of his condition. Amhara shrugged as a sideways grin slid across his face. His eyes moved in the direction of Commander Pho's men.

Following Amhara's gaze, Kandake's eyes roved over the battered faces of several of the men lined up before her. It was obvious that her friend had given better than he had received. She turned to Alara, scrutinizing every inch of exposed skin. There was no evidence of any more of the treatment she had witnessed.

"Please," Kandake asked of Commander Pho. "Unbind them."

Kandake embraced each one as their bindings were cut. The last to be loosed was Amhara. She stood in the space between Amhara and her brother.

"I have decided," the commander said, "that you will return to your home after we share a meal."

Shen said something that Kandake could not understand. His face was covered with unpleasant emotion.

"He said, 'You do not have the authority'," Alara translated. "He is saying that they have to wait for an overlord to make that decision," he continued.

"You understand what they are saying?" Kandake asked, surprised.

Alara nodded.

"I have the authority," Alara translated the commander's retort. Commander Pho pulled the wrapped stone from his pouch. He kissed it before he removed its fabric covering. He held it up for all of his men to see. At the sight of it, the men saluted and bowed their heads.

"Letting them go would be wrong. They killed four of our men," Alara continued interpreting. "They could be a danger to the Sovereign."

"I say they are not," Commander Pho countered.

"You cannot know that. What if you are wrong?" The man placed his hand on the knife at his side. "I will not let you do this. I invoke my right to challenge."

Kandake saw the heads of each man in the company swivel as one, moving to look at the challenger first, and then to the commander. Some of their faces held the same angry response as Shen. The others she could not read. Something important was happening. Alara's translation did not tell the whole story.

The commander bowed to Shen. His back was rod straight. All expression erased from his face. Leaving the assembly, he returned to his shelter. After a brief pause, Kandake followed. Receiving his permission, she entered.

The commander's face looked tired and drawn, quite different from the proud man with whom she had become acquainted.

"You are troubled," she said. "Are you that afraid of him?"

"Fear is not my problem," Commander Pho said. "While I carry this, it is wrong for me to fight anyone sworn to the Sovereign." His hand passed over the pouch at his waist.

"Cannot another fight for you?"

"They could," he answered, shaking his head. "Shen has always been a bully. And when he earned his rank, he became worse. He is a very skilled fighter. If they faced him and lost, he would not quickly forget that they stood against him. And there are those who agree with him. They would forfeit—concede to his position."

"And if you do not fight?" she asked.

"If I do not face Shen, I will be seen as a coward. I would lose my rank to him."

Kandake sat thinking. The commander's problem was as much hers. The consequences of a loss to the commander's subordinate meant that she and her brother would not return home. They would be trapped here and all of those with them.

There has got to be a way. I came here to make things better for Nubia. If I allow this to happen, things will be worse. If Shen wins, the best that could happen is that we stay here until an overlord comes. That is if one comes and if we are released. The worst is that Shen could decide that we should die.

Kandake's fears pulled at her. She felt herself drowning in them. In one last push of her will, she flattened them. *I will not squander Nubia's future in this place. There will be no offering tables prepared for our tombs, not yet. We* ARE *going home!*

"What are the restrictions of those who can stand for you?" Kandake asked.

"There are none," Commander Pho replied, shrugging his shoulders. "Protocol says that anyone I name can fight the challenge in my place."

"Then you will name me. Nubia will stand for you!"

45

"You cannot do this," Alara said, his voice pleaded as much as it demanded. "I will not let you." Alara turned to Kandake's friends. "Cannot one of you talk to her? Make her see why this cannot happen!"

Amhara and Ezena shook their heads. "We have already tried," Ezena said. "She will not listen."

"I offered to fight in her place," Amhara said. "But she will not accept that, either."

"You know that arguing with her is pointless," Ezena said. "When she makes up her mind, there is no changing it."

"Stubborn woman," Amhara muttered. "She will get herself hurt, if not killed."

Kandake continued to stretch and prepare for the upcoming battle as if she could not hear them. She took her time, making sure each muscle group was loose and her joints flexible.

Stones, laid in a circle, outlined the perimeter of the battlefield. It was set nearest the northern entrance. Shen stood at its center awaiting the arrival of Commander Pho. A soft breeze ruffled his hair. Sweat glistened on his skin. The sneer he wore resembled the snarl of a wild animal. The commander approached him, but refused to enter the ring.

"Are you afraid to face me?" Alara translated Shen's growl. "Good. Then things will change to the way they should be." He scowled at the Nubians standing with the commander. "They will remain my prisoners until the Sovereign sends someone to replace the Emissary."

"Fear has nothing to do with it! Tradition and protocol forbid me to fight with you while I carry this," the commander countered, indicating the stone.

Alara continued to interpret for the Nubians standing with him.

"If you do not face me," Shen said, "you forfeit your command to me. And then I will choose how to deal with the threat to our Sovereign." He turned away from the commander. "Pho is weak," Shen shouted to the witnesses circled around the stones. "He will not face me."

"You are right, I will not. But I have the right to name someone to stand for me."

The crowd hushed, waiting to hear which of them would have to fight Shen.

"Who would you choose?" Shen mocked, eyeing the men surrounding them. "None here would dare." He glared at his audience. Some shuffled their feet. Others dropped their gaze toward the ground. These men were eager to watch the spectacle, but all were more than reluctant to meet Shen in combat.

"I will stand for Commander Pho," Kandake said, stepping into the ring of stones. Her tongue tangled in the foreign words. Clad in her breastplate, she tied a square of rough cloth at her waist that wrapped her hips and thighs. She had slicked her exposed limbs with a mixture of oil and water to make them more difficult to grasp. Kandake stood facing her opponent.

"You would hide behind this...girl?" Shen said. His face twisted in a way that showed his low opinion of the commander and Kandake. He spat at Kandake's feet.

Kandake kept her temper under control. She would not allow this man's insult to rile her into making a fatal error.

Shen rushed at Kandake. His direct challenge displayed his lack of respect for her as an opponent. She waited until the last possible moment then stepped to the side. Kandake avoided Shen's attack with ease and used his momentum to push him to the edge of the ring.

"Your sister must be careful," Commander Pho told Alara loud enough for Kandake to hear. "If she angers him, he will certainly kill her with cruelty."

"What do you mean, 'kill her?'" Amhara asked.

"Although the challenge is not a battle to the death," the commander said, "if she disrespects him with mockery, Shen has the right to take her life."

Amhara flew at the ring. Only the quick responses of the commander and Ezena held him back. Kandake paused long enough to hold her hand up to Amhara, discouraging him from interfering.

The distraction gave Shen sufficient opportunity to make another pass at Kandake. This time he got close enough to cause her to stumble to the ground.

Shen dove for her prone body. Kandake rolled from beneath him just before he landed on top of her.

She used the energy of the roll to drive herself to her feet. Shen reached for her while he was still on the ground. Kandake kicked his hand away. The man was large and strong. His speed and agility were unexpected. On his feet in a flash, he grabbed her left arm and twisted it behind her back, hard.

Kandake speared the man with her right elbow, hitting him an inch below his breastbone. The shock of pain and instant expulsion of his breath forced Shen to release her.

The two circled each other. Waiting for an opening. Each studied their opponent, looking for any sign of weakness.

Shen made the first move. This time he appeared to be more wary of his adversary. He feigned to the right. When Kandake followed his movement, he plowed his powerful left fist into her stomach— driving her to her knees. The breastplate she wore would have stopped the point of an arrow, but the brute force of his blow was not hindered by it in the least.

Stars sparkled Kandake's vision. For a brief moment the world swayed as pain swept through her body. In an instant, Shen was on her. He stepped behind her, looped his great arm about her waist. Before he could drag her into himself, Kandake used his arm as a ledge to balance on, brought up both feet and pushed off of his abdomen. She flipped over his arm and landed in a solid stance in front of him. With her back to him, she glimpsed the pained expression on the faces of her friends.

Focus, she commanded.

Shen roared in anger. He lunged at Kandake as she turned to face him. He wrapped his arms around her, again. The strength of his grasp would surely break her back unless she did something.

She remembered the last time such a move was attempted on her. This time she refused to take a life to spare her own. Shen tried to lift her off the ground. Kandake circled her legs around his thigh. Using her heels, she battered the back of his knee until it gave way. The man collapsed under it. His fall broke the hold he had on her.

The pace at which Kandake moved challenged the eye that watched her. Rolling from his grasp, she had her foot at the back of the man's neck in one long stride. Kandake drove his face into the dirt. He grabbed her ankle, but she added more pressure until he loosed it.

"Concede or die!" Kandake said loud enough for everyone to hear. The strange words felt odd in her mouth.

When Shen refused to answer, Kandake pressed into his neck. Through the thick sinews, she could feel the fragile bones within it.

"Concede or die," she said, again.

"Die," came Shen's muffled response.

Kandake bore down until she felt the bones clicking against each other. She held him in that position until she felt surrender in his muscles. Then she released him.

"Nubia does not kill its friends," she said. Removing her foot, Kandake helped the beaten man to his feet. She dripped with sweat. Every part of her body ached. Kandake put her foot over the boundary created by the ring of stones with her back to the angry man.

She heard him growl and the gravel crunch beneath his feet as he approached. Shen moved quickly, but Kandake was faster. He came at her. Sidestepping, she allowed him to pass, hands locked together, and leapt into the air. Her blow met him, with all of her weight, at the back of his head just above his neck. Shen folded, mid-stride, landing in a heap at the warrior's feet.

46

The evening meal was made into as much of a feast as Commander Pho could make it. The commander's quarters were filled to overflowing with his Nubian guests. The floor had been covered with many hides to protect the food from the ground's dust. Platters of roasted goat meat and dried fruits were placed in the center. This was accompanied by a pitcher of water and another containing the off-smelling liquid, an aroma Kandake recognized.

The front wall had been rolled up and fastened at the roof, making it more of a pavilion. Pho's men were seated in comfortable groupings just outside.

Kandake searched the company, looking for Shen. She found him seated apart from the men, eating alone.

"Is Shen's seat meant as a punishment?" Kandake asked the commander.

"He eats alone at his own choice," Commander Pho said. "He usually eats with me, but you are eating here…." He shrugged.

Kandake nodded to Alara.

He left his food, walked the short distance to the commander's officer. "Princess Kandake wishes you to come eat with her," Alara told Shen in his tongue. "Please join us."

Shen opened his mouth to argue, but Alara's bright smile and respectful bow seemed to change his mind. Shen followed him without comment. He was seated next to Amhara across from Kandake. The feast was complemented with companionable conversation about cultural differences.

Throughout the meal, from time-to-time, Kandake caught Shen watching her. When she returned his gaze, he would flinch away as if expecting her to rebuke or rebuff him. Kandake took special care while they ate to include him, as best she could, in her conversation using her brother to translate. She told the story of how she became the next queen and her first thoughts and concerns about their grandmother's selection. Even Shen managed a smile or two.

"Princess Kandake," Commander Pho said around a mouthful of food. "We leave for Nubia at first light. The Sovereign will provide you an escort to ensure you arrive to Nubia unharmed."

"Thank you," Kandake replied, accepting his pronouncement as an attempt to mollify the original insults of their behavior. In the same vein, Kandake extended Nubia's good will to Commander Pho's ruler. "I would like to present your Sovereign with a gift to initiate relations between our two kingdoms."

She reached into the small pouch and removed several rings of gold. These she placed on the mat between them. Reaching into the sack again, she pulled the stone of gold-spangled midnight from the bag. This she placed in the commander's hand.

"This jewel is a symbol of friendship for Nubia." She turned it over, exposing the carvings on its flat side. "These markings signify the throne of King Amani, ruler of Nubia. But these new markings here," Kandake pointed to the grooves she had engraved with her knife, "indicate the reign of Queen Kandake." She closed Commander Pho's hand over the blue stone. "The bearer of this stone is welcome in Nubia throughout my father's reign and mine as well."

The commander executed a deep, respectful bow, his face not quite touching the ground in front of him. He explained to Shen what had just taken place, passing the stone for him to see.

"With your permission, Princess," Commander Pho translated for Shen, "it would be my honor to personally guard you to your home."

Kandake looked to Alara to be sure the answer she wanted to give was one that was within protocol. At his nod, she answered.

"It would give me pleasure to have you in my company," she said. "And knowing that your strong arm of protection is with me," she rubbed her sore middle, "brings great reassurance."

The man ducked his head at such high praise. Commander Pho thumped him soundly on his back and ordered more food and drink to be brought to them.

As the dining and celebration wound down, the band of Nubians made their way to the shelter that had once served as Alara's prison. They found fresh sleeping furs dispersed throughout the space. In the far corner set the pile of their belongings. Everything was there, including their weapons.

The front of their pavilion was rolled up to let in the night's warm air. No guards were posted to watch them. The stars of the darkened sky sparkled, showing them the way home.

The others in the shelter with Kandake lay down to rest for the journey that would bring them to the place of their beginning. But she was not ready for sleep. Thoughts scurried through her mind.

Kandake sat, gazing at the sky. She pondered all that she had accomplished—finding Alara and freeing him, returning him to Nubia, and possibly bringing with her the opportunity of a new alliance for the kingdom.

I have done what you have set for me, Great Mother. There were times when I believed I could not do it. There were other times I felt I would drown in my own fear. But like you said, I did what was needed.

Stretching, she moved her leg to a more comfortable position. The bells she wore at her ankle tinkled.

Being a warrior is what is right for me. Being queen is what is right for the kingdom. I can *do both. I* am *both.*

"I am what is right for Nubia," she told the stars. "I will rule it and I will protect it with all that I am. I am the next queen of Nubia. Queen Kandake, Warrior Queen of Nubia."

_47_

Kandake and all of the Nubians greeted the sun, mounted and prepared to return home. Commander Pho, Shen, and ten of his men formed an escort for Kandake and her party. Shen took up a position on one side of her and Amhara rode on the other. The group made one small detour to retrieve Kandake's supplies before starting their journey.

The first day of the trek passed without incident. Commander Pho's men served as a strong line of defense. He had two of his men riding point with them alternating as scout. Two of them brought up the rear of the party, providing protection. The others took up positions along their flank on either side.

As they traveled, Shen practiced what words he had learned of the Nubian language. They were garbled on his tongue, but he would not give up. He practiced until his words were intelligible.

"You are getting better," Kandake encouraged.

Shen gave her a shy grin and kept practicing.

Everyone took turns preparing the meals. The food was apportioned equally, but Kandake noticed that her meals always contained the best pieces of what was available.

"Would you like this piece?" Kandake said, offering to exchange her larger slice of dried meat with one of the commander's men. His was a much smaller portion. "I am not very hungry."

A grin spread across his face as he reached for the wedge of meat Kandake offered. Before his hand could wrap around the prize, he caught sight of Shen, glaring at him. The man demurred; he dared not accept it.

At night, Shen took care to sweep away loose stones before laying out Kandake's blankets. A watch of Commander Pho's men was posted while the Nubians slept. When Shen's watch ended, he slept near Kandake, ensuring he would be the first to reach her should there be trouble.

On the second day of travel, Commander Pho's scout returned to the group. As he reported to his commander, his speech was rapid and his demeanor excited.

"What is happening?" Kandake asked Alara. "What is he saying?"

"Something about a large company of riders approaching," her brother translated. "The commander asked if he could identify them. He says that they are still too far away."

"Could he tell what direction they had come from?"

"No. All he could determine was that they are headed this way and that they are moving fast."

Commander Pho shouted orders. His men separated the travelers into two groups. Kandake and Alara, along with her two close friends comprised one group and the remainder of Alara's hunting party made up the other. Kandake's band, accompanied by Shen and five men, was escorted to an area an appreciable distance away. They took a position on a small rise dotted with several trees, making it very defensible. The other group, along with Commander Pho and the rest of his men, stayed behind on the route they traveled.

"Now what?" she asked, dismounting. Alara exchanged a few quick words with Shen. Kandake heard her mangled name come from the large man's mouth. "What is he saying?"

"He says," Alara interpreted. "We wait here where you are safe while they find out who is coming and their intentions."

"No!" Kandake snapped at Shen. "I will not hide while others face danger for my sake." She pushed past her brother to leave the cover of the trees. The large man blocked her path, jabbering and bowing. She attempted to step around him. He moved to prevent her. Each time Kandake changed her direction, Shen intercepted her.

"Will you please tell him to move?" Kandake asked her brother, frustrated.

"He says it is his duty to keep you safe," Alara answered after an exchange with Shen.

"You tell him that I am going down there." She made a move to get around the large man, but he was in front of her again, jabbering. Kandake looked to Alara.

"He says that if you insist on going, he must go with you."

"Then tell him to get back on his horse." She turned to remount Strong Shadow.

"If he goes, so do I," Amhara said. "I am not staying here."

"Me too," Ezena chimed in.

"I guess we all go," Kandake said, throwing up her arms in surrender. She grabbed her horse's reins and vaulted to his back.

Closing the distance between the rise and where she had left Commander Pho's group, she saw a company of Nubian warriors. The armed men moved into an attack formation as they approached. Coming nearer she heard her uncle's voice shouting demands at Commander Pho. Uncle Dakká's arm was raised. The drop of it would signal the warriors to attack.

Kandake feared she would not make it in time. Pulling an arrow from her quiver she nocked it to her bow as she kneed Strong Shadow to a faster pace. From the corner of her eye she saw Shen do the same thing. She had no idea who Shen would aim for.

Kandake leaned forward as far as she dared, encouraging more speed from her horse. She placed her back at Shen's arrow and let hers fly. It landed at the feet of Uncle Dakká's horse. His head snapped in her direction. Her uncle turned toward her, bringing up his bow.

In a brief second, Kandake realized he misunderstood. Uncle Dakká pointed his arrow at Shen.

Not close enough to trust that he would understand her words, Kandake reeled Strong Shadow around. She brought him up on his hind feet causing a near collision with Shen's horse. The horses wailed their complaint. Shen leaned around for better position. Kandake brought Strong Shadow down so close alongside Shen that his arrow was snapped and his bow knocked from his hands. She hoped her uncle would understand what she was doing.

Wheeling her horse around, she saw that Uncle Dakká had dismounted and sited down the shaft of his nocked arrow. It was aimed at Shen. Natasen stood in front of their uncle with a hand on his arm, preventing a shot. Kandake slid from Strong Shadow's back and ran the rest of the distance. Shen and Amhara were less than two steps behind.

Kandake and Amhara came to stand before Nubia's Prime Warrior. They lowered their eyes in recognition of Uncle Dakká's position. Within seconds, Ezena stood beside her friend. The three young warriors placed themselves before their superior.

"Princess Kandake." Uncle Dakká pronounced her title and name with such precision that she knew there was displeasure in it. He stood before his niece, facial expression and voice identical. Both stern. "You are wanted in Nubia. That is the king's message and I have delivered it." His face allowed for a small hint of what could have passed for amusement, or possibly curiosity. "Young warriors, what have you been up to?"

_48_

"Report," Uncle Dakká ordered the young warriors. His face changed to an unreadable expression. The three friends exchanged sideways glances.

"My Prince," Amhara said. "Everything is as it should be." As the most senior warrior among the friends, the responsibility of accounting for their actions came to him.

"The Princess prepared to leave the kingdom to recover Prince Alara. It was not fitting that she journey alone. Ezena and I traveled in escort." He paused to see how Kandake's uncle responded.

"I see," Uncle Dakká said and waited for Amhara to continue.

Amhara proceeded in telling the tale from the time they left Nubia up to the time they were captured.

"Whose plan was this?" he asked Amhara without indication of approval or criticism.

"It was my plan," Kandake said. She described the path in detail and the wheres and whys of the placement of herself and her friends.

"Why then, did it fail?"

"Because of the unexpected," Ezena said. "They attacked our horses instead of us. By doing this they managed to unseat us, bring us to the ground, and overpower us."

"How do you come to be here?"

Kandake took up the telling from that point. She described how she was able to read and take advantage of her captor. She spoke of their exchange of information about their respective cultures and kingdoms and the release of her friends and Alara's party. When she got to the part about Shen's challenge of his superior and Kandake's battle with him, Uncle Dakká turned a hard, almost threatening expression toward the commander first, then toward Shen.

Throughout the three's recital of the journey's events, Shen had taken up a position near Kandake. He stood far enough away not to interfere or seem intrusive, but close enough that he was clearly within a protective range of Kandake.

Uncle Dakká turned to face the large man. His expression was no more than a raised eyebrow. Shen neither shifted his weight nor did he appear to be ill at ease. He merely bowed before the prince.

"Continue," her uncle said, turning back to Kandake.

Kandake resumed her tale, describing the feast, the gift of invitation to alliance to Commander Pho's Sovereign, and their journey home to this point.

Again, "I see," was all that came from him. Kandake's uncle seemed to study the ground at his feet. He stood unmoving for some time. No one in either party moved. Everyone waited in silence.

At length he raised his head, calling Alara to him.

"What do you think of these people?"

"I have been their 'guest' for more than a few days," Alara told him. "We were not ill treated, but their hand is strong."

Kandake searched her brother's face. She wondered if he remembered the blow he received, the one that she witnessed. She would not tell her uncle. It was for Alara to tell and if he was omitting it, he must have a reason. Kandake remembered her grandmother's words describing her brother as being slow to respond when others wronged him. *Or does he see something that I am missing?* In either case, Kandake remained silent on the matter. She would ask him later.

She turned her attention back to Uncle Dakká. She considered what he was contemplating. What conclusions would he draw? As if on cue, Uncle Dakká nodded his head in decision. He raised it and examined all who stood around him.

"We go to Nubia," he said.

Everyone mounted their horses and rode toward Nubia. Kandake and her band rode at the center of the group. Commander Pho and his men took up their previous positions as escort to Kandake. The Nubian warriors enveloped them all.

Shen rode closest to Kandake. He glared at anyone who broke ranks to speak to her.

_49_

The host of riders entered Nubian territory at its easternmost border. At the sight of the king's children, every citizen they passed cheered before bowing in acknowledgement.

Dismounting in the palace courtyard, Uncle Dakká sent a runner to notify the king of their arrival. King Amani burst through the doorway. As he stood at the top of the steps, Kandake saw him surveying the crowd. She and her brothers approached the stairs.

"My King," they said in unison. They dropped to one knee, with crossed arms over their chests, and heads bowed.

"My children," King Amani whispered. He took the steps in two long strides. Falling to his knees before them, he swept them into his arms and alternated between kissing them and weeping upon their necks. Queen Sake joined her husband in welcoming her children in their return. The king's kisses were no more than her own.

"Nubia celebrates," King Amani pronounced to the crowd that had gathered around them. "We commemorate the return of Nubia's greatest resources as soon as my children and our guests have been refreshed."

The queen instructed servants to arrange for lodging and refreshment for Commander Pho and his men. Shen resisted leaving Kandake's presence.

"I am home," Kandake told him in his strange words. "I am safe. Thank you. Please go with your commander."

"I go." Shen's words were heavily accented as he bowed deep and low. Shen followed as Commander Pho and his men were led to the warriors' compound.

Kandake entered her rooms and began removing her clothing. A slight rustling from a corner behind her pulled at her attention enough for her to grasp the knife she wore next to her skin.

"I see you have brought our brother back," Tabiry said. She pushed herself away from the wall she leaned against. "What I want to know is why you would bring those animals back here?"

"They are not animals They are human, the same as we are. Why must everything be a battle with you?" Kandake returned the blade before her sister saw it. *Some things never change.* Kandake blew out a cleansing breath and entered the bath without turning around.

"You still should not have brought them here," Tabiry said. Her voice dripped with disapproval. "What if they plan to harm us? Did you think about that?"

Standing in the center of the wide stall, servants poured vessels of clear water over Kandake's head and body. She scrubbed at her skin with a perfumed paste;

a mixture of animal and vegetable fats combined with salts and herbs. It felt good to get clean after the long journey and all that had happened. Her servants doused her with water again, removing the cream and the dirt with it.

Tabiry resumed her barrage of accusations.

I am enjoying this too much to be disturbed by you. Kandake focused on the feelings of the warm water being poured over her skin and of being clean. *I will not let you ruin my bath or any of the things I have done.*

The servants wrung the excess water from her braids, signaling that her cleansing was complete. Kandake dismissed the servants, preferring to dress herself. She carefully replaced Natasen's gift within her garments, having grown accustomed to having it there. Kandake stepped back into the main room, enhancing the jingle of the bells at her ankle.

"You are not Queen yet," Tabiry said, eyeing Kandake's foot.

"No, I am not," Kandake said, her patience worn thin. "You are my sister. I remind myself every time I weary of your constant aggravation." She strapped on the knife she wore at her hip and made for the door. But Tabiry intercepted her.

"You are planning to punish them for daring to take Alara, are you not?"

"I do not have any plans for them. That is not my place. As you remind me, Father is King. We would all do well to remember that." Kandake pushed past her sister and stopped in the doorway.

"You say that my 'warrior ways' will destroy Nubia. You would prefer that I give them up, spend more time with Aunt Alodia learning how to be tactful, cautious, *diplomatic*." She stepped closer to her sister. "To get Alara home I had to do *BOTH*, be both. "Great Mother made the right choice for Nubia. *I* am right for this kingdom. I am the queen Nubia needs."

Kandake spun on her heel, but not before seeing Tabiry's chin nearly meet the floor.

<u>50</u>

Kandake took her usual seat in her father's council chambers. Instead of King Amani seated at the head of the table, Uncle Dakká sat there in his absence. He presided over this meeting, making it a formal inquisition. He placed two Nubian warriors at the entrance to the room. Her uncle had also called for Kashta, Alara, and Natasen to be present while he interviewed Commander Pho and Shen about Alara's capture and the subsequent events.

Kandake looked around the familiar space. But things were very different this time. There were no servants or scribes present. No refreshments had been laid out on side tables. In a far corner, outside of the light, sat a lone figure. She peered at the person seated there. Squinting, she recognized the features of the man who had crept into her camp late one night. It was the man who carried Alara's bronze bell, Jarn.

To Kandake, Jarn still had the look of one that is hunted. His eyes darted from person to person, expecting danger, not knowing who would strike.

"Tell me, Commander Pho," Uncle Dakká began his questioning. "How is it you came upon Prince Alara?"

Uncle Dakká's eyes were fierce. The expression on his face was hard, as if it had been etched from ebony. Kandake had seen her uncle angry and stern with warriors who had disobeyed an order or some other infraction, but never had she seen him like this. The danger of his bow, the edge of his knife, and the threat of his bare hands were summed up in the tone of his voice—cold, hard, and humorless.

"My men and I were scouring the area, looking for my superior officer and my Sovereign's Emissary." Commander Pho spoke with both hands splayed upon the tabletop, a clear indication that he had no intention of grasping a weapon. "We found their bodies, along with those sent along to protect them, among the brush not far from where the prince hunted." The commander's eyes took on the hardness of iron as he spoke.

"My superior officer and the men with him died in battle, but they are soldiers. That death is expected; they are honored in it. The Emissary was beaten—his body was broken and mangled. He had been robbed and left to die in a strange land. The Emissary is not a soldier; there is no honor in his death."

Commander Pho paused. He stared at a scene that only he could see. Seated near him, Shen dropped his gaze, staring at the table.

"Jarn," Pho indicated the man in the darkened corner with the jutting of his chin. "He was the only one of the party left alive—and only just barely." He shook his head and continued. "We were angry. We searched for the perpetrators of such an evil. That is when we came upon Prince Alara and his hunting party."

The commander blew out a long breath. As the air left his body, so did his dignity. Kandake noted that Commander Pho diminished with the telling of what had happened.

"I asked Jarn if these were the men who would dare such an atrocity. He said that they were not, but I refused to believe him. You have to understand that the Emissary was a learned man. He was a man of knowledge, not a soldier such as we are. And his servant would be expected to know less than he about battle and men who kill. So we assumed that Jarn was afraid to tell us the truth. He told us and we refused to listen. Our anger—my anger, did not want to believe him.

"So we took the prince, and those with him, back to our camp. We convinced ourselves that he was guilty of this crime."

"When did you decide that the prince was innocent of this offense? What convinced you?" Uncle Dakká asked.

"I believe I always knew," Pho said. Sitting at the table with Kandake, he seemed only a shadow of the man she had begun to know. "But when Princess Kandake came to our camp to rescue the prince, she began the erosion of the wall that I had named truth. Her strength, her conviction of what is right—her honor shamed me. I could no longer deny what I knew to be true."

"Yet you required that she fight this man before you would free them." Kandake's uncle spat the words from his mouth. Pho shrank even more. He opened his mouth to speak.

"That is not true," Shen said, speaking just above a whisper. "That was my doing." His words came at a tortured pace. His heavy accent and his newness to the language mangled the meaning of the words to the Nubians around the table.

"Allow me to help you," Alara said to Shen. "You speak and I will translate."

Shen nodded his agreement. He made eye contact with Kandake's uncle. He held his gaze while he spoke. "When Commander Pho said that he would release them," Alara translated, "I still needed someone to blame. So I challenged the commander, knowing he could not accept it. Then I would gain his rank and I would never let them go." Shen returned his gaze to the tabletop.

"Anger is a very dangerous thing," Commander Pho said, shaking his head. "It has brought us to a place of shame and dishonor."

"And you found no sign of the ones who truly attacked your Emissary?" Uncle Dakká asked.

"We found only the weapon that we left with your guard at the door," Pho said. At Uncle Dakká's signal, a warrior standing guard at the entrance brought a parcel, wrapped in a rough woven cloth to Uncle Dakká. He laid it on the table in front of him. Her uncle unwrapped it. What lay before them was the same type of weapon found on the bandits that had attacked them in the grove.

Kandake felt the sharp edge of cold rage enter her stomach. She pushed it away and focused on what was being said.

"We had hoped to find more of these among the young prince's possessions, but there were none." The commander shrugged his shoulders and resumed his gaze upon the table.

"I see," Uncle Dakká said. "You may leave us now." He had Shen and Commander Pho escorted back to the warriors' compound. Jarn went with them.

"What do you think of his story?" Uncle Dakká asked Kashta.

"If what he says is true, these are not the men responsible for the attacks."

"Prince Alara," Uncle Dakká's eyes rested on Kandake's oldest brother. "Has this man told the truth as far as you can say? Has he left anything out of his account of his treatment of you?"

"I believe him when he says he did not really think we had done this. While we were being held, he would not allow the others to mistreat us, and there were those who wanted to and would have, if given an opportunity."

"Princess Kandake, do you have anything to add?" her uncle asked.

"No, My Prince, he has told the truth as far as I can tell you."

"Then we are adjourned. I will give the king my judgment."

Everyone rose to leave and filed out of the door. Alara and Kandake were the last ones to go through.

She took hold of her brother's arm and drew him back into the room.

"You did not tell Uncle about Pho hitting you. Why?"

"You saw that?"

"Why did he do it?"

"He asked us where we thought the Emissary's servant had gone. I told him Jarn had gone to tell the truth to those who would know truth when they heard it. And because I used his own language so that everyone would understand what I said, he hit me."

"But why not tell Uncle Dakká?"

"You heard what Pho said." Alara paused, held his sister's gaze with his own. "Anger is a dangerous thing."

51

Kandake sat in the meeting with King Amani and her uncle within the council chambers. She listened as Uncle Dakká explained his conclusions from his interview with Commander Pho and Shen. She noted that he took great care in his wording of her fight with Shen, but the way her father looked at her, she could tell he was not pleased.

"You do not think these are the same men that have been attacking our caravans?" the king asked.

"It does not appear to be the case, My King."

"You do not think they pose any threat to the kingdom at this time?"

"No, My King. But the warriors are keeping an eye on them."

King Amani considered his brother's words. He turned to his daughter. "And what are your thoughts on the subject, Princess Kandake?"

"I believe it is as the prince says, My King. He has warriors watching Commander Pho and his men. If there is a danger, they will intervene."

"And the feast?"